SWEET
CONFESSIONS

SWEET
CONFESSIONS
EROTIC FANTASIES FOR COUPLES

Edited by
Violet Blue

CLEiS
PRESS

Published in the United States by Cleis Press, Inc., 2246 Sixth Street, Berkeley, California 94710.

Printed in the United States.
Cover design: Scott Idleman/Blink
Cover photograph: Pando Hall/Getty Images
Text design: Frank Wiedemann
First Edition.
10 9 8 7 6 5 4 3 2 1

Trade paper ISBN: 978-1-57344-665-5
E-book ISBN: 978-1-57344-686-0

Contents

INTRODUCTION: EROTIC EXPOSURE AND THE THRILL OF THE CHASE

To have sex, one of you is going to have to be the one to say, "I want to." As much as we'd sometimes like to avoid that scary moment, it is inevitable. If we want to get to the good stuff, we have to be vulnerable, even just for a second.

It is a risk whose rewards far outshine the possibility of an unwanted outcome. When you're with someone who makes you feel that crackle of electricity, that lust that gets under your skin and sinks to the meeting point of your most vital parts and stays there—when you're with that person you know you can ask for maybe just a bit more. You feel it. It's a circuit of arousal and erotic inspiration that flows when you make contact: skin contact, eye contact, heart contact.

It turns "I want to" on its head. It means you might be able to ask for something you really want, something you never got to ask for before. New fantasies come with hot sex, heartfelt love and true lust. But confessing a fantasy is a moment in time that must be savored: you must devour it like a cool, sweet fruit on a hot summer day.

The couples in this collection are so well crafted, they feel as real as someone you might know—but they are so very sexy, they're more like the people you see one place or another that you *want* to know. I worked with talented and well-known writers to make sure of it. I wanted no dark scenarios, but real, vibrant and layered erotic stories featuring complex, surprising and believable characters —people whose confessions would feel like your own.

The stories are outrageously sexy—and they break the mold in literary excellence. Explicit sex is folded into sexual fantasies for couples in a way that puts you right there in the action and makes you want to come back for more. I was astounded at the emotional honesty, the talent, and the jaw-dropping sexual scenarios in theses stories.

I hope they inspire you to fess up.

The heroine in Heidi Champa's "Smell As Sweet" turns classic office life into a riveting scene. An accidental discovery reveals a woman's handsome coworker has a weakness for women's panties, and she leverages his confession into an endless supply of expensive lingerie, ravishment atop desks and a woman who knows how to make a strong man confess. There are the best kind of "Bad Influences" in Devyn Christopher's luxurious hot tub encounter, where the members of a loving couple confess to wanting a woman who can strap it on, and a man who loves to be sexually owned. Turnabout happens in Kayar Silkenvoice's "Internet Café au Lay," in which a rugged, ever-hard boyfriend gives in to his girl's desire for semipublic sex, with an urgent encounter that left this editor breathless.

Sexual confession can be a wicked game. "Silver Screen," by Portia Da Costa, is so delicately crafted, you're put in the female protagonist's unusual and uncomfortable situation—a woman in an X-rated theater—and we don't find out until the twists and turns complete whose confession made the filthy anonymous hands jobs impossibly possible. A young woman from East London combines her sexual confession to a boxing instructor with the vulnerability of love's first heated sexual consummation, but not before a bare-knuckle takedown that will leave scenes from "The Contender," by Jacqueline Applebee, ringing in your head and other parts long after the story is finished.

When we think of confessions, we tend to think of places of worship; Sophie Mouette's "Sacred Places" puts an incredulous Catholic girl into a Welsh monastery where her boyfriend wrenches profane confessions and orgasms out of her in equal measure. Unforgettable, "Counterpane," by Alison Tyler, brings us into the world of a drop-dead sexy man who whisks his lover out of the office for her lunch break, where they greedily devour lust by the spoonful in her confession-made-reality of double-time in a hotel room with two hot men.

"Waisted," by Angela Caperton, is a Cinderella story of corset fetish sex; a lush female point of view festoons this tale of male control in which a woman is restrictively dressed and then driven in a black limousine, and finally plundered by her lover's generous anatomy deliriously and desperately on a plush carpet while bound in expensive tight laces and brocade. On the flipside of female desire and fetish, "Underpants," by K. D. Grace, shocks and surprises when a man dresses his lady for sexual ravishment, but she's taken aback at the bizarre knickers he makes her wear out to dinner for a cat-and-mouse game of turn-on and arousal that surprises everyone.

"Red," by Piper Morgan, begins with a confessed fantasy that seems mundane but grows into deftly revealed outrageousness and gripping erotic tension as the desire to experience a real-life erotic fairy tale morphs like a wolf under a full moon into a deliciously depraved sex game in the woods. Often the couple's shared fantasy is to fuck a stranger: "The Hotel," by Anika Ray, is an ultrarealistic playing out of that scenario between an aggressively nervous couple—with a surprising and very hot ending, proving that sometimes it's better when things don't go as planned.

Lingerie and admission of sexual fantasy go together like satin and lace; the saleswoman in "Underwear," by Kay Jaybee, gets more than she expected doing a home delivery of items for a man who's so sexually forward she doesn't believe he actually has a girlfriend to buy underwear for. That is, until the two women meet and turn panty sales into a game of sexual one-up(wo)manship. In "All Shaved Up," by Liv Olson, a playful yet shy woman admits she likes shaving; her naughty boyfriend admits it too, as they take turns daring each other to smooth down and go further.

"New Day, New Life," by Andrea Dale, drops us into Prague, where a woman is celebrating a renewed outlook on life with her loving man; an outlook that includes admitting her desire to try sex with another woman—a gorgeous Eastern European woman, in a threesome as explicit as it is loving. An American erotic romance writer goes to the United Kingdom for research and winds up in "An Age Play" of her own in Regina Kammer's hot story of an older woman, a young man's first lessons in oral sex, and a very understanding husband.

When erotic confessions come true they are inevitably accompanied by uncertainty; Alexander Liboiron's "Are You Sure?" exquisitely explores a woman's confessed need to be roughed up during sex—but the taboo that makes both of them blush and their hearts race is the reason she wants it.

Jenna wanted it; only because Eric loves and accepts her completely can she go through with it. "Jenna's Gambit," by Jeremy Edwards, plays on a girl's fear of being caught relieving herself in public, twisted into a heightened erotic experience by a man who loves her, understands the eroticism of humiliation, and knows how far a couple can go when they feel safe to do the nastiest thing one of them can imagine.

"The Female Gaze," by Rachel Kramer Bussel, is a show-stopper of sexual confession and romantic lust and risk, gorgeously playing out one of the most popular emergent taboo fantasies of our generation. In it, a girl's boyfriend is ogled by women and men in equal measure, but it's what the boys want to do to him that gets her head spinning and her pussy thrumming. Realizing her secret fantasy is the same filthy scenario, she cruises a gay bar for them both—with a resulting sexual encounter that is as satisfying as it is surprising and unforgettable.

This book is a collection of confessions and fantasies so realistic that you could, in fact, try these at home. But whether you enjoy these privately, get a little bit of inspiration or share them with someone special, I hope you will take hold of your fantasies and promise to try a sweet confession—at least once in your life.

Release your desires to the one you love, and give chase. I promise you won't regret it.

Violet Blue
San Francisco

SMELL AS SWEET

Heidi Champa

I sat down at my desk, the ease of the weekend long gone as another week loomed large in front of me. The work I had left behind was still waiting for me, but so was another gift from Jamie. I got up and closed my door, wanting privacy for reading his instructions. The panties inside the envelope were pink lace and silk La Perla, cut low on the hips. The note that sat on top held just a few words. I read it quickly before doing anything else.

Hope you like the Wild Orchid panties as much as I do. Wear them all day and come to my office at five.

The quivering jolt of naughtiness went all through me as I slid off my own panties and slipped on the ones he wanted me to wear. I paused briefly to let the silky softness rub over my legs, before settling them into place over my moistening cunt. It was going to be another long day at the office, but things were certainly looking up. This was the first time Jamie wanted me to come to his office and not just to leave the panties and go. I was intrigued and couldn't wait to find out what new adventure Jamie had planned for me. Our strange arrangement started accidentally, but had quickly become a regular routine. A late night at the office a few months ago had started the whole thing.

That night, the offices were quiet, but the stack of papers in front of me didn't seem to be getting any smaller. I kept glancing at the clock: the time was moving quickly, but the work was going at a snail's pace. It was already way too late to meet the girls for the dinner we had planned; they would soon be off barhopping and making merry. All I had to show for my evening was paperwork—useless forms and reports—and a looming deadline for first thing Monday morning.

As I slogged through, there was finally a light at the end of the tunnel. I closed the last file folder and let out a sigh of relief. The joy proved short lived when I looked at the clock and realized it was near midnight. I thought if I hurried, I could meet the girls at the last bar of the night and have a quick martini to reward my hard work. Grabbing a stack of folders to drop by Jamie's office, I whipped out my phone and started texting Charlotte to find out where the action was. Too busy clicking letters with my thumbs, I nearly walked into Jamie's office door, which was open, just a crack. I saw a dim light and heard weird noises coming from inside.

Getting even closer for a better look, I saw Jamie in his chair, his cock in his hand. I froze, my fingers stopping midtext as I opened my eyes wider at what I saw next. There was a pair of black panties over his nose and mouth, the crotch pressed right against his skin. His dark hair was covering his forehead; his eyes were pinched shut. He inhaled deeply and loudly, twice, before he came, white come spilling onto his fist and the floor. I hurried away before he could see me, taking the elevator down with my heart still pounding.

I got into my car and raced to the pub, unable to shake the image of Jamie with the panties on his face. He had seemed in seventh heaven when I saw him sniffing the lace-covered crotch. Shaking my head, I crinkled my face in disgust. Fetishes rarely surprised me, but this was one predilection I'd never heard of. At first, I was dying to let the girls know what I had found, but as I downed my perfectly chilled vodka concoction I thought better of it. I just wanted to forget the whole thing and enjoy my weekend.

The problem was, I couldn't forget it. No matter what I did, the visual of Jamie kept coming back. I went over every detail in my mind, from the sound of his cries to the thickness of his cock. I struggled to understand what it was about the panties that he liked so much. I had always assumed that most men weren't all that fond of the way a woman smelled. Lord knows there were enough feminine hygiene products on the market to tell us so. But he seemed so lost in it, so enthralled by what he was doing. I thought all men jerked off to porn or at the very least a picture of someone naked. The pure pleasure he got from those simple little panties seemed to trump any naked woman for him. Could smell really be that powerful, that erotic? I had honestly never thought about it before. Now, I couldn't stop.

I lay in bed Sunday night, my mind again consumed with Jamie and his desires. I wondered whose the panties were; who would go along with such a thing? No doubt they came from the Internet, some stranger trying to make a buck. I then wondered what he would think of my scent, if the smell of my pussy would turn him on as much as the black lace panties did. Without thinking, I reached down and pulled off my own panties, bringing them up to my face. Inhaling my own scent, I wasn't disgusted at all, but I wasn't turned on either. It wasn't as if it was the first time I had smelled myself, but now I tried to imagine what Jamie was thinking as he did the same thing. The thought of him and those panties, how hot they made him: now *that* turned me on. I wanted to be the one with the power, the one whose essence filled his nostrils as he came. Monday morning couldn't arrive fast enough for me.

I got to work early, clutching the small bag in my hand. Making a quick detour to Jamie's office, I dropped my present on his chair and got out quickly. I didn't leave a note, just the panties. If he didn't freak out and run to HR, I would approach him after work and reveal the truth. The charge running through me was palpable; my body was alive with anticipation and fear. I tried to work, but I kept my eyes out for Jamie's arrival. As much as I wanted to stake out his office and see his reaction, I knew I couldn't. I took a few deep breaths and picked up a folder.

The afternoon wore on, and I saw Jamie several times walking the halls, looking the same as always. I don't know what I was hoping would happen, but I knew by now he would have found the panties. Would he wait until he got home to sample them, or would he use his office again for some after-hours fun? The hours went by slowly, but finally the end of the day arrived and I waited for the herds to leave Jamie and me alone. He didn't get onto the elevator, so I knew he was still in the building. I was trembling as I walked to his office, still not knowing what I was hoping to find. When I arrived at his door, his eyes were looking down, and the panties sat on his desk, still in the plastic bag. I gave a small knock and entered; his eyes met mine, a blush rising in his cheeks. Glancing at my panties, I sank into the chair and waited.

"You want to explain this, Liz?"

"Explain what, Jamie?"

He slid back in his chair and regarded me with distrust. His arms were crossed over his chest and he looked defensive. God, he still looked so cute, though. His dark eyes pierced right through me as he watched me, trying to figure me out.

"Well, I came in this morning and found these on my chair. I also happen to know that you were here late on Friday, just like me. It had to be you who left these. Now, if you saw something and are trying to be cute, I'm not amused."

I tried to be cool, but I knew my face was giving me away. I didn't speak at first, trying to compose myself. But he pressed me, not letting me off the hook.

"Admit it, Liz. You were spying on me. You saw me on Friday. And now you're trying to mess with me."

"Okay, fine. I saw you. But I'm not messing with you, at least not in the way you think."

"So, what? You thought this would be funny? It's not funny, Liz."

"It's not supposed to be a joke."

"Then why did you do it?"

I sighed, not wanting to tell him the truth. But I didn't have any alternative.

"I couldn't stop thinking about it all weekend. Watching you with the panties, well, I was intrigued. I wanted to see if mine would have the same effect on you as the pair you had on Friday."

Now it was my turn to blush. He didn't speak, just ran his finger along the edge of the plastic bag containing my lavender panties. I watched him move to open the bag, but his ringing phone stopped him cold.

"I've got to take that, Liz. Maybe we can finish this conversation tomorrow."

He left me no choice but to nod and leave his office, unsatisfied with his response to my boldness. I was hoping for something more, but I was left with the horrible feeling that I had ruined a relationship with a coworker for nothing.

When I arrived at work the next day, I expected Jamie to avoid me completely. I didn't see him as I got off the elevator and when I walked by his office, it was empty and dark. I went to my office and closed the door, slumping into my chair with defeat. But I jumped up immediately when I felt something under my butt. I was stunned by what I saw: a small paper bag. When I opened it, I saw them. Red and tiny, the panties were not what I usually wore and appeared too brief to cover much of anything. There was also a note in the bag, and I opened it with trembling fingers. In simple script, it had a profound message.

You smell amazing. Wear these for me today and leave them in my office at five.

I couldn't believe my eyes. The words on the page sent a shot of fresh moisture to my pussy. It was exactly the response I had wanted from Jamie. Now that the moment had come, all my apprehension was overtaken by desire. I slid my own panties down from under my skirt and stepped out of them. The red panties were definitely not my style, but if it was what Jamie wanted, I was willing to oblige him.

As I put them on, my body registered the tiny slip of fabric between my legs. Without any other stimulation, my pussy continued to get wetter throughout the day. The idea of handing over the flimsy thong to Jamie at the end of the day, and of him pleasuring himself to my scent, consumed my mind during every task I performed that day. I didn't do anything out of the ordinary; in fact, to the naked eye my day was as boring as any other. But inside my head, the flow of desire built all day long. As I sat at my desk, waiting for the hand on the clock to slide to five, my panties were damn near soaked through. In a few short minutes, I would leave the panties for Jamie in a plastic bag, waiting for him to unseal and take a whiff. What at first had seemed so strange to me now seemed only hot and forbidden.

As I slid the panties off, I couldn't resist a quick inhale. My scent was pungent, just like it always was when I was deeply aroused. I set the panties discreetly on his chair and made my way to the elevator, waiting for Jamie's next move.

Now, after months of handing off panties to this man, I made my way to Jamie's office at five, just as he had instructed me to. The pink panties were still on as I sat in the chair across from his desk and waited. After leaving him numerous pairs of panties, and indulging in countless hours of fantasy, something had finally changed. I stiffened a little when I heard him come in; his hand rested on my shoulder before I saw him. He sat down across from me and smiled, laying his hands flat on his desk.

"Thanks for meeting me, Liz. You're probably wondering why I wanted you to stick around today."

"Yeah. I mean, usually you just want me to leave the panties. They're beautiful, by the way. You have great taste."

"Thanks. I had something else in mind for us today. The last pair of panties you gave me were fantastic. It's amazing how much your scent changes from week to week. And unless I'm mistaken, this last time you seemed particularly, um, excited."

My face flushed crimson as he leaned farther toward me. I uncrossed my legs and felt my pussy clench at his insinuation. It was amazing how he could tell, just from my scent, his effect on me.

"You're right. I was. This whole thing is driving me crazy."

He smiled and stood up, walking over and towering above me.

"That's what I figured. So I thought maybe today we could do something about that."

He took my hand and led me around his desk until I was leaning on the edge and he was standing between my legs. He hiked up my skirt, exposing the gorgeous pink panties. The wet spot right over my cunt had grown, and he smiled again when he saw it. He pushed me back gently until I was lying on his desk with my legs spread wide, my heels resting on the edge. He looked down at me before he dropped to his knees, his head right between my thighs. I waited for something to happen, but there was only the sound of his heavy breathing, deep inhalations ringing out in the silence of his office. His fingers traced over my puffy lips, our skin separated by the moist fabric. He brushed over my clit and I gasped at the contact. He stood, his hands running down my legs as he spoke.

"I want you to make yourself come, right in those panties, Liz. I want to know how you smell after you come. It's all I can think about. Can you do that for me?"

Without a word, my hand dropped to my cunt, and I started rubbing myself through the sodden fabric. My clit jumped under my touch, and I couldn't stop myself from crying out. I looked at Jamie and saw him opening his pants before he sat down. His hand was around his hard cock and he sat back and watched me, stroking himself gently as I rubbed myself harder and faster.

"Jamie, I'm going to come. Oh, god."

My eyes couldn't stay open any longer and I closed them tight. My body shook on his desk, pushing papers and folders to the floor with my convulsions. As my tremors started to subside, Jamie's head dropped to my pussy, and he breathed deeply of my scent. He came as he smelled me, my sweet scent pushing him straight over the edge. His free hand rested on my leg as he shook; his face twisted in pleasure as he took one last whiff of me before he slumped back into his leather chair.

I sat up and looked at him, spent and happy. Slipping off the pink panties, I laid them gently on his desk. I stooped to kiss his forehead, still sweaty from our exertion.

"See you tomorrow, Jamie."

"Bye, Liz."

As I reached the door, he stopped me before I could go any farther.

"Hey Liz, next time, I'm thinking boy cut. What do you think?"

BAD INFLUENCES

Devyn Christopher

I was in my bliss. I slept past nine, finished the tawdry novel I had been reading, enjoyed the sun while the dog chased seagulls along the lakeshore and was about to join the sweating glass that awaited me near the hot tub. I could not have imagined a more perfect way to cap last night's happiness.

He had invited friends, family and even some of my coworkers to surprise me for my birthday. He arranged for a wine tasting, and the sommelier (a tall Australian in a cobalt, Italian silk suit) introduced my very impressed family to excellent varietals as we nibbled on a decadent display of cheeses. I savored each taste of aged grape, blending them on my tongue with Quebec Oka or French Camembert until I felt my eyes flutter behind the lids.

He wasn't in bed when I awoke, and the bedroom had that damp, sweet scent of a freshly showered man who had been up early and was already dressed. The house was quiet. I donned a robe, and by the time the aroma of good coffee reached me, I saw the note on the kitchen table and the small truffle beside it. Nice.

Happy birthday, you fucking drop-dead gorgeous hottie you, the note read. *Sorry: got urgent email this morning, need to run into the office. No crisis. Ain't I a good company slave? Everything from last night already tidied up. Mostly. Have a great morning, see you in a few. Love you tons!*

It was already midafternoon when I slipped into the tub, and it wasn't long before I felt the splash as he joined me after coming home. I smiled from under my Ray-Bans. He gave me a kiss and dunked himself before stretching out across from me. I enjoyed the view of his wet arms as he ran his hands over his head, slicking back his hair.

Jason is definitely eye candy, with a radiantly happy face under a golden crown, the kind of legs that only a passion for soccer could sculpt, a chest to match and an always-positive attitude. And a handful of cock that swayed heavily above a pair of tight, smoothly shaven balls.

"Great party, huh?" he laughed, as he turned on the jets.

Enjoying the streams against my lower back, I looked at him from across the steaming roil of bubbles.

"Remember Shannon from my work? I can't believe you invited her! She's a riot, isn't she? The little wench." Shannon and I had been sharing the same cubicle for the last year, and between her confessions during smoke breaks and the things she let me read before she texted them to her lover in Phoenix, my libido had become more and more appreciatively inspired.

Most of my friends were pretty straight laced; Shannon stood in stark contrast to them all. My grandmother would have called her a bad influence, which very probably would have meant we would have become BFFs had we met in college. She hosted adult novelty parties on the side, selling sex toys to successful, suburban women who had their hands in their pants while their husbands or boy toys or screaming kids were out of the house. I'm by no means a fragile or inexperienced flower, but never before had I heard of some of the things she had available: Miniature vibrators that fit on the tip of a finger or looked like a tube of lipstick. Tiny metal cuffs that comfortably, but unyieldingly, clamped around the thumbs. And my favorite: the L-shaped dildo that sported a pretty blue phallus sticking forward like a real dick while the other end was slid inside you. That thing made my imagination run wild.

"Isn't she the one who you said fucked the intern?"

"The bike messenger. They went out for a while, but she got tired of his bullshit. I think she was just hot for the image—the piercings, you know? God knows he was a change of pace for her."

He laughed. He has such an amazing smile, my guy. I paused, remembering a moment from last night when my coworker swayed into me in the hallway. She was hammered and tugged on my forearm as she chuckled and whispered in my ear.

"Lucky bitch," she had slurred. "He has one fucking delicious little ass."

"What are you thinking about?" he asked after a moment, seeing that I had retreated into my head. I smirked and sipped my drink, relishing the frothing water around us, feeling my muscles loosen as we languished together under the afternoon sun. I cocked my head at an angle to show a little attitude before responding.

"Baby, have I ever told you that you have a great butt? Even Shannon thinks so. She told me last night." There was that smile of his again as he stood up, the dripping water shimmering like jewels down his chest and abs in the light. His dark swim trunks clung around the soft but delightfully thick penis that I knew lurked underneath them. His cock is as beautiful as his smile.

I am a lucky bitch.

Two small steps across the hot tub and he was standing imperiously before me, like a robust Olympic athlete fresh from the pool. He bent downward and kissed me, holding my face in one hand as the other pushed wet hair back from my brow. His lips tasted sweet and warm, and I languished in the shadow made by his broad shoulders as if a special, private curtain had been raised around us. I felt the flutter and the tingle. I raised my hands to his calves as the kiss continued and kept them there after he slowly withdrew and stood straight up again. He grinned appreciatively.

"Well, sir, you do!" I reached up and under the trunks and grabbed myself some handfuls of husband. He laughed again, but gradually stopped and grew quiet when I kept my hands where they were, cupping his asscheeks and squeezing them softly.

So many times had I watched him in the shower, or playing soccer, or jogging on the beach, and found my eyes simply riveted to the sculpture under his lower back. Smooth and pert, Jason's ass had the lightest touch of blond peach fuzz running down his spine, into the sexy crevasse underneath and along each firm bun. I loved holding his ass when I sucked his throbbing dick, pulling him into my mouth with it.

I bobbed my outstretched palms and fingers on his flesh, feeling his bubble shape and patting him. His ass filled my hands nicely. I slowly drew a finger or two up and along the seam between his cheeks, enjoying how pert he really was. Daringly, I slowly probed a finger inside farther, found his anus and teased it with a fingertip. It was warm and soft and tight, and I exerted a little pressure under the very outermost ring of his sphincter when it started to clutch the tip of my finger.

My arms still around him, I felt him tense up as he pulled back just slightly. The quizzical look on his face was precious.

"Um. What are you doing?"

Did I see the hint of a smile under those widened, glittering eyes?

"I'm enjoying my man," I smirked, looking up. I pressed my forearms firmly against his strong legs and held him, my hands sending a clear message: stay just where you are, dude.

Did I feel a sudden swell against my chest?

"You've had too much gin," he laughed, as he tried to pull away. I gripped his ass even tighter, pulling him firmly enough against me that the bulge under his trunks was just above my shoulder. I held him in place and delivered a crisp, splashing smack.

"I'm drinking iced tea," I said with a saucy smile.

I felt my belly tense and my heart skip a beat. I knew I was at the threshold of uttering something that I had been deeply desiring for a while. To utter it out loud would be to somehow make it more real, to commit to it. Had I intended to really do this, here, now? But here I was, with him before me and his yummy butt in my hands, and it was time for me to either lunge forward or slink back into a place where I would keep this only to myself.

"You are a lucky bitch," she'd said.

Unlike some men from my past, Jason had always been supportive of my choices. It's a big reason why I appreciated him when we started dating, and it became a fabulous part of what we had built by the time we were married. I trusted him, and that's really what made me lucky. Somewhere deep inside myself, I knew that if I really expected him to be intimate enough with me to actually give what I wanted, I'd have to be brave enough to open up about what I was after, what I had been masturbating about for so long. I took a breath and chose to move forward. I chose to press my luck.

My saucy, playful grin must have shifted into something closer to stern concentration and hungry desire, because as my eyes bore into his, his jaw went slack and, from under him, I could easily see his breathing quicken.

"Turn around for me, baby. I'm not going to hurt you. Do it."

Yes: there was a definite swell in those trunks now. Any other time, with me sitting on the ledge against the hot tub jets and him standing before me, I'd happily reach into them and withdraw his velvety cock for a sucking. Part of me wanted it in my mouth right now, to feel its girth widen my lips and my tongue swirling around his bulbous head, but there was something I wanted, had wanted for so long, to have even more.

Slowly, quietly, he turned around. His wet, muscular back glistened in the bright sun, and I tried to calm the thunder in my chest as I ran my hands up his spine and around his waist, feeling him, adoring him. The roiling bubbles splashed along his hard and rounded calves, but the view of his thighs was spoiled by the way those trunks crinkled and clung unattractively around them. I decided to remedy this.

Teasing myself, I ran my fingertips along the small of his back before curling them just under the elastic waistband. Jason stood perfectly still, knee deep in the hot tub, as I started to lower his trunks. When the seam between his cheeks revealed itself to me, I pressed my face close to his hot skin and rained tender kisses there. I darted my tongue across the crack of his wet ass, feeling the shape of him with it, as the trunks were tugged lower and lower until they were finally crumpled under his behind.

I leaned back. I turned off the jets, and the water gradually stilled around us as I languished in the sight of my man's perfect ass displayed before me. I felt incredible. Why had I waited so long, denying myself this moment, this pleasure? He is my husband, my man, and this beautiful ass of his is part of the deal. I felt like a queen of Egypt examining a newly acquired Greek slave for my own visual entertainment. I felt like a divine goddess casting approving judgment upon a male of the species whom I had just fashioned out of clay.

Spreading my fingers, I gripped Jason's ass widely and slowly squeezed until I could squeeze no more. I caressed him, smacked him, petted him, swirled my palms along his rib cage and down the breadth of his thighs before squeezing him again. Jason stood delightfully still, looking down at me from behind a shoulder, and then I noticed that his right arm was moving slowly.

From someplace within me that I had rarely, if ever, felt before, I heard a stern tenor creep into my voice.

"Just what do you think you're doing?" I was the queen, a goddess, the keeper, She Who Takes Her Pleasure. You are mine. You will obey. You will serve my desires.

"What?" He blinked his eyes a lot and stopped.

"Get those hands of yours off my dick." I gave his right cheek a loud, open-handed smack. I felt supreme. "Got that? My dick. Now bend over a little, boy. Put those hands to good use on your knees."

Jason tried to smile but any attempt at being sarcastic or making light of this was already a lost opportunity. His hardness revealed his commitment. He looked confused, and his eyes darted in every direction, but soon he found himself leaning forward slightly and resting his hands as instructed. I squeezed both cheeks and spread them open.

Three years of marriage and never before had I really seen his anus; not like this. His smooth, honeyed skin contrasted with the auburn ringlet that crinkled around the tight rosebud before me. His full and tender balls hung handsomely in a round and firm sac, with the skin between them and his asshole simply begging for light caresses. Water beaded and dripped from his balls and the few manly hairs between his legs. As I sat behind him, still waist deep, I cupped those delicious balls in one hand as I brought my face to the crack of his ass and pressed it there, sliding my tongue between his sac and back door. He spread his legs wider for me. He groaned.

I held his cheeks open again and darted my tongue across his warm, soft, inviting rosebud. He quivered and I could feel that his cock was twitching as it jutted forward into the sun and just over the water. My cunt was thrumming as I feasted on him, feeling my face pressed close. I wanted out of the tub.

I stood up with a splash. Wrapping an arm around his chest, I made sure my breasts were firm against his back as I looked over his shoulder to enjoy seeing how intensely stiff he had become. I wrapped a hand around his cock and tugged on it like a leash.

"Come on, you," I stated firmly and led him into the house, up the stairs and into the bedroom without ever letting go of it. He was speechless. When I gently pushed him into the adjoining bathroom, I grabbed a towel and threw it at him before stripping off my own swimsuit.

"Dry me, boy."

Jason remained silent, and the look on his face was somewhere between trepidation and desire as he dropped his knees to the ceramic tile to run the soft cotton up my legs. He stayed there as I turned for him to dry my back. I reached behind myself, tugged his closely cropped hair, and brought his face to my cunt as I bent over and spread my legs.

"Lick me."

Immediately, his tongue swabbed my swollen lips in wide, slow strokes, and I felt his face press right up against my asscheeks. His jaw tilted up and forward as he started to search inside my pussy, and I squatted for the best angle to grind my hardening clit against his chin. I used his face, and I could hear him gasping for air as he struggled to keep balance with his hands on my ankles.

When I stood again and turned around, his face was glistening with my juice, his eyes were wide in anticipation, and he was panting. The wide head of his handsome cock...my handsome cock...bobbed against the cold tiles in gentle taps with each deep breath he took. It was almost purple and had swelled wider than I had ever seen it before, a silken mushroom bulb on the end of a deliciously thick, smoothly cut and throbbing stalk.

I decided it was time to play with my dick. I grabbed a handful of his hair, tilted his head back, gave him a hard and full open-mouthed kiss, and yanked him to his feet. He complied unsteadily and submitted to my lead when I directed him directly in front of the sink and the huge mirror above it.

"Hands down. Bend forward. Stay still." His ass looked so inviting.

I grabbed some lubricant from a bedside dresser and, back in the bathroom, stood behind him. My cock was standing tall, its head just barely touching the edge of the counter. I pressed my tits close to my man's muscular, bare back and caressed his chest while using the mirror to look into his eyes from over his shoulder. He stared back at me, panting.

Reaching around his waist, I coiled my fingers around the girth of that beautiful thing with my left hand and gave it a few slow, teasing strokes. My cock was swollen and warm, still slightly damp, and twitched like a live animal in my fist. Jason closed his eyes and groaned, his head lolling to one side. I let go and scooped an overgenerous palm full of lube into both of my hands.

Jason was still bent over slightly, and his eyes popped open again when he felt a wet fingertip from my right hand slip between his tight buns and gently dart around his asshole again. He blinked nervously but stayed quiet, took a breath, and looked at me. I kissed his back. I whispered as I tickled the rosebud between his firm cheeks.

"Just relax, baby. It's okay. You're beautiful. I've wanted to do this for a long time."

He steadied himself and yielded, pushing his ass backward and against my fingers. I felt a surge in my cunt and a flutter in my belly as his anus began taking the tip of my finger into his warm tightness. Darting the fingertip, I moved his muscles in slow circles, opening him gently, pressing forward slowly, until eventually I had two fingers inside his body. He was gasping for air and wobbled as he felt his knees weaken, and when I brought my other, drenched hand around my cock again, he moaned loudly.

My cock was hard as stone as I tugged on it, jacking it off faster and faster now. Just hearing the loud, squishy jerking and my man's staccato moaning had me close to cumming, but I wouldn't have dreamt of reaching for my clit now. I was pumping his ass, fucking him. *I was fucking him.* I fucked Jason with long strokes now, my fingers deep inside of him, as I jacked that cock off harder and harder. It was steel in my fist, quivering, and when my grip focused just around the wide head and stroked it in short, tight, rapid pulls, it swelled even wider and tenderly. My left arm was a blur as my right steadily and deeply pistoned my fingers inside him, my boy, my slave, who was shaking now with his head almost touching the mirror. The glass became foggy with his labored, panting breath.

His tight buns slapped against my hand sensually as I fucked him, and I loved watching his sexy, smooth asscheeks ripple ever so slightly after each pounding stroke. Unable to help himself, he thrust his pelvis forward rhythmically, taking my fingers even deeper inside him and giving my pumping grip even more of my thick cock to enjoy as he did so.

His mouth was wide open in forbidden ecstasy. His eyes were screwed tightly shut. His shoulders rose and dropped. His anus began to tighten and squeeze around my pounding fingers when he stomped a foot and began to shake.

I felt my cock twitch and spasm, and gripped it tighter as I stroked it. I rubbed my wet thumb along the underside of the head, enjoying the satin feel and contours of it. Jason started to scream then, and as my fingers fucked him long and hard, as I gripped my cockhead, I felt a sudden splash against my palm. Jet after jet of thick, creamy manhood filled my hand as my cock started to burst. Jason swayed against the sink, his legs giving out from under him, and I pressed against him harder to keep him standing.

He gasped and opened his eyes, looking into the mirror and my own. We stood still together, and I savored the sight, my hand still firmly gripped around the wet truncheon before us. I nipped his shoulder gently as I slowly withdrew my fingers and his chest surged forward slightly. His eyes still bore into mine. He was still panting. I stroked the penis gently and slowly as I felt it begin to wind down, softer now but still thick and beautiful in my grip. He swallowed and stood straight. I smirked.

"Well," I whispered into his ear. "My birthday gets better and better."

"Oh, my god," he whispered back, finally pulling away to start the shower. "That was…"

I couldn't find the words either.

"Let's throw another party. And let's invite Shannon again… she has something to show us that I'd like to try."

His quivering kiss was all the response I needed.

INTERNET CAFÉ AU LAY

Kayar Silkenvoice

The throats of the orange-red flowers seemed to swell as they drank greedily of the sunlight's golden sweetness. My eyes tracked a couple of bees flirting from blossom to blossom, slipping deep down the flowers' throats to gather that sweetness for themselves, only to emerge seconds later, launching back into the air in search of the next source of nectar.

Glorious day, I thought, as I closed my eyes and let my head loll against the back of the chaise. I could feel the breeze tickling my skin, teasing the sun-kissed flesh, making my nipples harden. Sighing, I shifted a little and licked my lips. The sun was making me hot and the wind was making me hotter. I found myself wondering how I could entice my lover into the shadowy interior of the beach house for an afternoon of lazy lovemaking.

"Are you ready for some food?" Kurt asked from somewhere above me.

I lazily opened one eye and spotted him.

"Mmm. Lunch. What a good idea," I said, thinking how providential it was that his stomach decided it was empty in the same moment I'd decided I needed filling.

I lifted my hand and he took it, pulling me upward, out of my chair. I leaned into him and slipped my arms around his waist. I pressed my lips to the skin exposed by the V of his shirt and inhaled sharply. His unique scent commingled enticingly with the salt tang of the air, flooding my senses. I slid my hand down his arm and taking his hand in mine, stepped toward the house.

"Life's uncertain. Let's have each other for dessert, first."

"Oh, no you don't," he tugged back. "I said 'food,' not 'fuck,' you insatiable wench."

I pouted at him, then smiled, realizing we'd be going inside to eat, and once there I could use my hands and mouth to convince him to feed me what I wanted—bent over the kitchen table. My clit twitched at that mental image and a small shiver ran through me. But he knows how my mind works, Kurt does. He smiled down at me, and there was a slightly cruel edge to his voice when he spoke.

"We're going to Seabiscuits," he said, naming a busy little place that was a combined Internet café and lunch stop. He knew I liked their finger sandwiches, iced coffee and free wifi.

A bead of sweat formed between my breasts and hung there, trembling with each beat of my heart, each breath, making me extremely aware of my skin, my breathing, my pulse.

My need.

Just as I was preparing a protest, my tummy grumbled. I rolled my eyes and capitulated. He crooked his arm at me and I looped mine through his, and off we strolled toward the main street of the little beach town.

As we walked past kite shops and candy stores the wind flirted with the hem of my sundress, which worried me a bit, since I wasn't wearing anything under it. I decided to pretend I was wearing a thong, a mental trick to keep me from feeling too exposed. Not that I mind being exposed, but I prefer to initiate it myself, from a playful space.

Kurt noticed, of course. I figured the bounce of my breasts caught his eye. "I thought you had your swimsuit on under that," he said with a bit of a frown.

"No, I just threw it on when I got out of the shower, remember?"

He nodded, and we continued walking toward our destination. Hot and thirsty, I picked up the pace, which made my breasts bounce even more under the loose-fitting sundress. My nipples rubbed against the fabric, which made them hard, and which in turn made my clit twitch. It is a blessing and a curse, having sensitive nipples, and this was one of the cursed times. The friction was heightening my arousal, and I knew Kurt would make me wait. My past lovers wanted me to come quickly and often, but not him. He is perverse that way, making me wait, keeping me on edge sometimes for hours, until I am mindless with the urgency of it and begging for release.

Preoccupied with such thoughts, I would have walked past our destination if Kurt hadn't given me a tug on the arm. We stepped into the blessedly cool, dark interior of Seabiscuits and goose bumps immediately pebbled my skin, making my nipples tighten even more. I ordered a tall glass of iced coffee and triangular little finger sandwiches with wasabi cream cheese, cucumber and avocado. Kurt ordered salmon teriyaki and a pint of the local microbrew, and we sat down at our usual table, where the tabletop is inlaid with a checkerboard for playing chess or checkers.

We are well matched at chess, Kurt and I. We rarely ever finish a game, because they often go out thirty or forty moves and that can take hours. So we play for the love of it, and to polish our opening moves.

On this day my mind was not on the game, and I made a stupid move with my king's knight that cascaded into me losing badly. Not that I minded losing, but Kurt was grinning far too widely, relishing the fact that he'd mated me in fourteen moves. So when my king surrendered, I decided to get my revenge, determined to mate with him in less time than it took him to checkmate me. I figured I had about thirty minutes.

While I was trying to decide on my next course of action, I picked up my glass of iced coffee. It was rather slippery, beaded as it was with moisture, and as I struggled to maintain my hold on it, a bit of the liquid spilled on the tabletop. I mopped it up with my napkin and went to get a fresh one.

On the way back, I sat on his lap and slipped my arm around his shoulders. I brought my fingers up to squeeze the back of his neck. He closed his eyes and made a sighing purr. I shifted ever so slightly on his lap, pressing my mound against the front of his shorts. He tilted his head back and looked at me through narrowed eyes.

"Is that appropriate here?" he asked. I could tell by his tone that he thought he knew the answer.

I let my gaze wander the café. There was a young couple reading books on the bright red couch near the storefront window. He was sitting, and she was reclining with her head pillowed on his thigh. A gaggle of college-aged girls were seated around a circular table, their faces avid and their voices low, punctuated with giggling outbursts that caused the boys at a nearby table to look nervously their way. The boys were playing a role-play card game and they appeared to have demolished a hefty lunch, based upon the number of plates they'd stacked up and pushed aside. Two elderly men, dapper, sun-browned and stoop-shouldered, argued amiably over a game of checkers. And finally, three solo males, each with laptops that they seemed intent upon, completed the scene. I don't think any of the patrons had noticed me sitting on Kurt's lap, and if they had, they'd not skipped a beat.

I leaned forward until my mouth was close enough to his ear that my breathy moan could only be heard by him. I tightened the cheeks of my ass and wriggled it. In response, I felt something in his lap twitch. I gasped into his ear and leaned into him, pressing my breast more firmly against his chest.

"Kay..." he said, warningly.

I looked into his eyes. I smiled slowly and squeezed his shoulder. My fingers played with the muscles there. Kneading them.

Needing him.

"Kurt," I purred back at him. "I have something to tell you."

His cock thumped against the front of his shorts, causing the fabric to stir against the lips of my bare sex, already slick with juices. I let the fingers of my other hand tease his collar as my eyes scanned the room. Every place my eyes alighted, a delicious vision came to mind. I wanted him to lean me over that table, there, where those college girls giggled, and fuck me hard and fast. Oh, imagine their shock! The round O of their mouths and eyes as they witnessed pussy plundered by cock! I wanted to sit on the edge of the sun-streaked couch and pretend to read a book while he buried his face between my thighs. I imagined myself standing on the table where the older men played their game, bumping and grinding my hips, the hemline of my dress riding up my thighs. What a commotion that would create! My pussy clenched at that thought, but I decided to settle for a discreet snake dance, instead.

"Scootch forward a little, would you?" I asked him.

"Why?"

"So I can ride you once I've gotten your shorts unzipped."

He froze, closed his eyes, and sighed. "Are you out of your mind?"

I just looked at him with lust-glazed eyes.

He shook his head at me and said, "We should go."

I grinned wickedly and twisted in his lap so I was straddling him. The sundress rode up my thighs, and they glowed whitely in the semidarkness, my plump thighs did, splayed as they were over his own khaki-clad ones. My hands gripped the back of the chair for balance. "I want you here, Kurt. In the café."

Something changed in his face. The glimmer of amusement faded. "No," he said. "I don't know about you, but I don't want to get arrested."

"Oh, the police wouldn't arrest me," I said airily.

"No? What makes you think you are immune to charges of public lewdness?"

"The police would never arrest me because I can't come quietly." I said, grinding my pussy against his erection as I enunciated *can't come quietly.*

He groaned at my bad pun, then grinned reluctantly. "When I get you home you are going to be in so much trouble, you evil wench." His hand lightly slapped one of my asscheeks.

I squirmed in his lap; caught his eyes; saw that he was serious. He wasn't going to budge. Very well then. I looked back at him, a level look: cool, calm, collected. The dance was over, the board cleared. Time to let the king know exactly what he was going to sacrifice...

"I don't want to wait until we get home, Kurt. I want you here—now—or not at all." *Check.*

His head jerked back a little. Now I had his full attention. I'd made a bold move with my queen. He could take her, or flee.

"Just who would that be hardest on?" he hedged, his eyes flicking a look at the tight nub of my nipple. His expression was fierce, and it thrilled me.

I met his gaze and defiantly ground myself against him. *Queen taps king. Check, your move, remember?* "You appear to be the hard one," I answered.

And with that, he made his move. He frowned deeply and half lifted, half pushed me off his lap, setting me on my feet. I pouted at him, thinking that my gambit had failed, but my pout quickly transformed into an amused grin. Kurt gave me a quizzical look and I pointed to the slick wet spot on the front of his shorts. His hands fell from around my waist and slapped against his thighs. He cursed under his breath and glared at me.

Once again my eyes searched the café as I pondered our predicament. Then it came to me. Yes! The perfect solution.

"Stand up and follow close behind me," I told him.

"Why?" he asked. His suspicious tone hurt a little, but I knew he had every reason to suspect that I was up to something.

"Why? Because the restroom here provides an air-blower to dry hands instead of towels. We can use it to dry that wet spot on your pants. Or we can sit here and wait for it to dry naturally..."

He nodded and stood, taking a position right behind me, his hand resting on the back of my neck. I found myself shivering under the warmth of it, under the control he exerted over me with it. He followed me to the restroom, one of those big, unisex, handicap-accessible bathrooms done in tile. With a relieved sound he made a beeline for the hand-dryer, and while he was preoccupied with trying to position himself in such a way as to focus the hot air on the front of his shorts, I smiled triumphantly and locked the door.

I pulled my sundress over my head and hung it on the hook on the back of the door. I'd said I wanted him here, in the café, or not at all, and I'd be damned if I was going to pass up this opportunity to get my way. Warmth flowed through me at that thought, and juices welled up between the seam of my labia, staining my inner thighs.

I sauntered over to the sink and stood before it, thinking it would make a good prop for what I had in mind. It was a long, low sink that jutted out a bit at thigh-height. Mmm...perfect! I leaned over it and put my hands on either side of the cold porcelain. My nipples tightened and I shivered at the contact. I cleared my throat rather loudly, and when Kurt turned to look at me, I met his eyes in the mirror.

The expression on his face was classic, and as soon as I saw it, I knew I'd won.

"You are soooo bad," he said as he moved toward me, already unbuttoning his fly.

I wiggled my ass at him and he gave it a good slap that made me yelp a little. The tile surfaces magnified my voice and reflected it back at us.

"Shh," he said as his shorts dropped and his warm hand splayed over my sacrum, holding me in place.

I could feel his weight shift and the heat of his cock pressing against me. He gave a hard shove and I hissed at the shock of it, at the feel of his head forcing its way into me, always a tight fit no matter how wet and ready I am.

I watched us in the mirror. There was something powerful in the juxtaposition of my naked, bent form and his clothed torso towering over me. I looked so vulnerable in that position, which exposed the long pale curve of my back to the bright light overhead, and the knuckles of his hands were visibly gripping my hips, holding me captive. I could see myself leaning over the sink, my breasts pointed downward, my nipples hard, so hard and long, just aching to be tugged on. I watched, too, as my breasts began swaying in time with his thrusts. It was very hypnotic, that swaying motion, and I watched it for some time before I switched my focus to Kurt.

My study of his reflection showed that his head was bent, his eyes focused on that place where our bodies joined. His shirt was bunched up a bit around his waist, to keep it out of his field of vision. I wondered if it looked as good to him as it felt to me, the long slow slide of him stretching me open, the cling of my inner labia as he pulled back. At one point he pulled me hard against him and pumped deeply into me, his head thrown back and his eyes closed. I moaned and he shushed me as it echoed in the little tiled room. I tried to be quiet, but when the violent rocking of our bodies together caused my hips to slam into the edge of porcelain sink I was braced against, I cried out with pleasure and pain. It was erotic, hearing myself that way, hearing the bright echo of my cry, and I stopped trying to be quiet. In fact, I was downright noisy. I rode out my pleasure on the cock that impaled me, and I let myself give voice to it despite Kurt's admonitions to be silent so as not to be overheard by the other guests of the café.

"Is this what you wanted?" he ground out his question between clenched teeth just moments after a particularly brutal thrust had made my eyes fly open and my breath catch.

"Yes!" I gasped, and then added somewhat defiantly, "And it's—about—fucking—time!"

In response, he forced my legs farther apart with his own and tangled his hand in the hair at the back of my head. He tugged, pulling me upward, and the shift in stance positioned my mound so that every thrust of his hips ground my clit into the edge of the sink. It sent pleasure-pain jolts through my body, and it was not long before I was coming, my pussy clenching and unclenching around his cock, my mouth open as gasps and moans and cries were wrung from me.

"Come for me," I implored him as I rode that tide of pleasure, and he bent himself to the task. His eyes closed and his fingers tightened in my hair and he hammered himself into me hard and fast until finally he froze and emptied into me with a long, low groan. As his cock twitched inside me he pulled me up against his chest and took a breast in each hand. He sank his teeth into my shoulder and rolled my nipples, making me quake inside and out.

God, I love this man, I thought to myself, because despite his prudery about sex in public places, I could always entice him to indulge me. I reached my arm back and pulled his head down toward me. I kissed him, sucking on his bottom lip, scraping it with my teeth as I let myself relax into him.

"Don't get too comfortable," he said, stepping away from me. I grabbed the edge of the sink for support and watched in the mirror as he walked to the door and took my sundress off the hook. He wiped himself off with it and then tossed it at me.

I spun around and caught it, then gave him my best indignant look.

"Kurt!" I gasped. "I have to wear this!"

"Yes, you do." He smiled at me, a short meaningful smile. "Consider it the price for getting your way." *King mated,* he acknowledged.

I laughed delightedly and gave him a slow smile of my own.

Yes, I supposed, *a come-smeared sundress was a small price to pay for a café au lay.*

SILVER SCREEN

Portia Da Costa

I t's a grubby little backstreet cinema, and it smells grubby too. My nose wrinkles at the pungent aroma, an unsavory potpourri that I don't really want to analyze.

Sit on the third row, on the right, in the middle of the row, he said, giving precise instructions, as always. I peer into the flickering chiaroscuro gloom, my belly fluttering with nerves as I search for a vacant seat. God, I hope there aren't *too* many perverts in the specified area! A few, I can handle. Too many and the peril outweighs the fun.

My Harry can be a bit too much sometimes. His games are wild and his orders even wilder. But I can no sooner disobey him than stop breathing or feeling.

Trying not to draw too much attention to myself, I creep down the central aisle. My heart thunders. It's a grim, grimy, horrible place, but still it excites me with its miasma of sexy sleaze. I imagine unspeakable things going on down every row. There is an usher on duty who's probably far more entertained by the show in the auditorium than the one on the screen.

The shadows seem to heave with activity: Fumbling. Fingering. Fucking. All the things, or at least some of them, for which Harry has commanded me to come here.

Shifty movements circle my peripheral vision, and I thank god that the light from the screen is dim and defective so I don't have to look at anything too closely. In the muggy, flickering murk I can imagine my own world, my own cheap and nasty scenario in this cheap and nasty place.

The gasps and groans on the stuttering soundtrack don't muffle the gasps and groans from the theater itself, and its scattered clusters of desperate patrons. Clandestine ecstasy is like a gathering vapor in the air, as strong and affecting as all the other, less salubrious odors.

I feel a clench, deep down low, at the thought of unknown bodies rocking together. It's a frisson that's both sick and irresistible.

Above me, the film plays on. A couple bump and grind, buck and moan. They're infinitely more athletic and somewhat more stylish than the patrons slumped and jerking in the scummy, never cleaned seats, but I doubt that they're enjoying themselves a fraction as much as my viewing companions are. But then again, who knows?

Part of me wants to look away from the screen, but that kind of sex is like a car crash. You just have to look. And when I do pay more attention to it, I almost laugh. The guy who's putting it noisily to his pneumatic brunette companion looks vaguely familiar. He reminds me of Steve, a buddy of Harry's. My demonic boyfriend constantly teases me about liking his friend and has been badgering me for ages to admit that I fancy fucking him.

And now, when I've finally admitted it, *this* is what he does.

He sends me to a porno movie where the lead actor looks just like Steve. Well, not exactly like him, but near enough to create a luscious empathy.

And the way Fake Steve is gripping his partner's hips even reminds me of Harry's own favorite sex style.

He likes to grab me and really shove into me in a rough, relentless doggie-fashion. And I like to be grabbed and shoved into, I must admit. Especially when he's growling a long, low rap of outrageous filth into my ear and plotting one of his mad, outrageous schemes.

Like this one.

Reaching the third row, I slip in on the right side. Oh, yuck, my shoe instantly squelches in some unidentified substance underfoot. I've a shrewd idea what it is, and judging by the gasps from across the aisle, quite a bit more of it is about to be deposited any moment now.

The place is so utterly filthy and sleazy, yet it makes my pussy flicker with a perverse, delicious longing—for Harry, dark Harry and his dangerous touch.

Where are you, you unmitigated fuck?

He has to be around here somewhere. He hasn't phoned me to cancel, so the game is still on. I feel light-headed, high on a cocktail of danger and a melting wash of yearning.

Curious eyes turn my way as I slip into the prescribed seat. My heart pumps, my hormones surge, pure lust wells up.

My clit throbs like a heart too, calling to Harry, as my panties flood with juice.

I want to rubberneck around, looking for him, but now I'm in my seat, that's forbidden. I have to keep my eyes completely focused on the screen, watching the action scrupulously as I pretend to allow a "stranger" to feel me up. Watching every bump and grind of the performers as I perform too, for this "stranger."

Harry loves for me to be slutty, and this is the ultimate in sluttiness: playing around and making free with myself in this dark yet public place.

I sense a presence moving toward me. Someone slides in at the end of my row. It's not busy in this section, and soon he's worked his way along the seats and is sitting right next to me. I hear the faint creak of a leather jacket, and I'm glad he's here at last. It's taken him long enough. I was starting to feel vulnerable and not in a good way.

But now it's game on. I smell a sexy male cologne, something strong and woodsy that punches its way through the fetid smells around me and makes my head feel light. It's not Harry's usual brand, but then, I wouldn't expect it to be. That would be a dead giveaway. It's yummy though, and its narcotic odor seems to send all the blood in my body rushing straight to my genitals. My breasts feel heavy, the nipples hard and crinkled inside my bra, almost painful. My pussy feels slippery and bloated and the temptation to slide about in my seat and stimulate myself that way is unbearable. I try a little wriggle, attempting to knock my clit against the gusset of my knickers, but it seems to make things worse, not better.

Beside me, however, my stranger emits what just might be a sigh of appreciation. Wiggling and waggling around in a dirty cinema seat isn't doing a whole lot for me yet, but it's certainly hitting the spot for him all right.

Up on the screen, the ersatz lovers have changed position. Fake Steve has pulled out, and his lady friend has turned over. She's rubbing herself enthusiastically, squirming about on the satin sheet, her thighs flung wide while he looks on, handling his more than ample cock.

Is Real Steve that big?

I wish for a moment that I was on a bed such as that one,

a vast arena with acres of room to maneuver. While both my "stranger" and Real Steve looked on, I'd lie back, lift my knees and hold myself open, blatantly displaying my sticky pussy to them in glorious Technicolor and aching detail. I imagine dazzling film lights shining down on it, warming it from without as lust warms it from within, revealing every last crinkle and crevice of my sex lips in merciless high definition.

As Harry...sorry, the stranger...edges closer across the imaginary playing field of the black silk sheets, I insert a finger inside myself and Real Steve slides close on the other side, groaning in appreciation.

There's a groan from my right now, and god, I want to look around. Has the stranger got his cock out? Has he preempted me? Hell, I'm slacking. I haven't really done a thing yet apart from wriggle around a bit in the darkness.

Desperately aroused and almost hyperventilating with fearful excitement, I ease open my jacket, then stealthily unbutton my blouse. There's a rustle from beside me, as if my companion is having trouble with his equipment and has been forced to adjust his position again to give himself some ease.

So...maybe he hasn't got his cock out after all?

Having dressed carefully for this jaunt, I easily flip open the front fastening of my bra, nudge aside the cups and let my boobs swing free.

Oh shit, I've done it now. I've shown myself. This is the public risk that Harry dared me to court. Because I can't look around to check, I can't be sure who's watching. There could be dozens of punters ogling my pale breasts gleaming in the light from the cinema screen, a whole cadre of men who're scrutinizing my exposed nipples, edging forward in their seats in the hopes of seeing either me, or the stranger beside me start to fondle them and play with them.

In for a penny, in for a pound, I think, as I oblige, having to bite my lips at the silvery jolt of sensation that speeds instantly from my nipple to my clit.

I'm a powder keg of lust, ready to go off at any moment. My eyes almost cross, but with my few remaining fibers of self-control, I focus on the screen.

Fake Steve is holding himself in his hand and rubbing up and down the inside of the brunette's long, shapely thighs. His buttocks flex as he moves back and forth, back and forth. The dark girl swirls her hips as she plays with herself, moving in a surprisingly graceful syncopated rhythm.

I go on pinching my nipple hard, emulating the rough but thrilling way Harry likes to handle me. Even though I can't look to the side, I can close my eyes and imagine Harry plaguing my breasts, pinching and twisting, while Real Steve reaches between my legs, combing through my pubes until he finds my clit and pinches that too.

Tears of frustration squeeze from between my tightly closed lids, and I bear down, grinding my aching pussy against the less than immaculate seat cover. It's no good, I'm going to have to touch myself down there and come, or I'm going to have some kind of seizure, that's for sure.

I'm just about to pluck at my loose skirt when a hand from the right beats me to it. I almost wet myself I'm so shocked, so thrilled. Still pulling at my tit, I shift my thighs, open them wide as the hem eases the fabric up and up and up and pretty soon my pussy is exposed. A great waft of pungent woman smell drifts up, almost drowning out both my stranger's delicious cologne and the scents of the cinema itself. I lift my bottom, helping him to ease my skirt from beneath me, and the sleazy degradation of sitting bare-assed on the filthy seat almost makes me come.

For a moment his hand covers mine, squeezing my breast,

then it dives down again, slipping into my pussy, just as Fake Steve's plunges into his babe's pussy, up on the screen. He starts to pump her with two stiff fingers, just as two stiff and very broad fingers jab magisterially into me. I whimper softly, then stifle the sound with my free hand. A thumb squashes down hard on my clit, and then with a rhythmic pincer movement he works me roughly, without mercy.

I bite my hand. My heels scrape the filthy floor. The muscles of my thighs and buttocks tense to the point of pain. I bear down on the ruthless grip that beleaguers my entire sex.

It takes just moments for me to come like a freight train.

I gasp and heave for breath as I come down. And just as I'm about to shatter the game and turn and give Harry a sloppy kiss for his kinky efforts, his hand, still scented from me, presses firmly against my cheek, forcing me to remain focused on the screen and the rise and plunge, rise and plunge of Fake Steve's hips and bottom as he vigorously fucks his fake lady love.

So, the game has to be played to the end. It's time for quid pro quo.

I hear the sound of a sliding zipper, and then a big warm hand takes mine and conducts it to a big warm cock. Dear god, does he want me to kneel down amongst the condom wrappers and the months' and years' worth of dried semen on the carpet and suck him? Even while I cringe, my pussy flutters again at the thought of it.

But no, he just folds my fingers more closely around his penis and begins to use them as a glove, working up and down, up and down, sliding easily and slickly on his precome.

It seems to take an age and my arm starts to ache. But all the while my pussy's aching too. Rubbing him makes my excitement surge again.

He sighs now and again, but still he doesn't say anything.

Those are the rules, even for him. Even when he comes, saturating my fingers with what seems like an ocean of semen, he barely gasps and then recovers in seconds, zipping up and rising abruptly to move away along the line of seats.

Wham, bam, thank you, ma'am.

I sit motionless for a moment; then, in an embarrassed, sweaty flurry, I bring myself off again. I have to.

Afterward, still shaking, I set my clothes to rights, almost leap to my feet and stumble from the cinema in a daze.

The trip back to Harry's flat is a compete blur. I'm assuming he wants me to go there and meet him afterward. We haven't spoken since he laid out his wicked plan two days ago. When I finally reach my destination, I let myself in, looking forward to a large glass of wine while I wait for him to get back too.

But something's wrong. There's a presence in the flat. Wine forgotten, I fly through to the bedroom and find Harry there, bundled beneath the covers in his huge wide bed, with books and tissues all around him, and glasses and cups and an open box of cold remedy sachets on the bedside cabinet.

My face must be a picture. He laughs and wheezes. "Sorry, babe, couldn't make it. I've got a cold." The way he's smirking though, despite his red nose and watery eyes, tells me that he knows that I still went, all the same.

You bastard, you could have phoned!

"But...but..." I quiver with a combination of horror and renewed arousal. What have I done? It's willfully dangerous, letting myself get masturbated in a public place, by a real stranger. Yet I'd do it again if I got the chance; I just couldn't help myself.

"Don't worry, love, it wasn't some tramp or free-range pervert or other deadbeat who brought you off, you know." He plays his fingers languidly over his mobile phone that's resting on the counterpane amongst the sickbed detritus.

But just when I think he's going to call someone, there's the sound of the flat door opening and closing, and then a firm tread approaches the bedroom. When it arrives at the bedroom door, and even before I turn around, I get a whiff of a luscious and now familiar male cologne.

There's the soft creak of a leather jacket, and as I slowly face its owner, my heart and my pussy flutter, newly hungry...

At the sight of *Real Steve*, handsome and smiling and ready to go again.

THE CONTENDER

Jacqueline Applebee

U ncle Ray was a boxer long before I was born. Ray "Magic-Hands" Harris was a big, stocky man; stern with strangers, but an absolute sweetheart to his friends. He was also a first-class cook. I remember standing on a chair when I was little so I could watch him make bread. He would pound the sticky dough with his powerful fists to create something amazing. Ray's not exactly a contender nowadays. Sure he's still a big man, but the leanness of his stomach has turned flabby over time; the strong muscled arms that used to swing me round and around have grown thinner, slacker.

"I can still kick your arse!" he would call out when I would try to do something for him. "I'm not dead yet!" What Ray's body had lost, his mind had retained. He could still go the distance when he was being a stubborn old git.

I became a single parent when I was nineteen. My son, Blake, who is my simultaneous ray of sunshine and royal pain in the bum, wanted to be the heavyweight champion of the world when other children wanted to be astronauts or explorers.

I went to pick Blake up from a boxing club in Bethnal Green. The Victorian building was stuffy, sweaty with male bodies who danced about in and out of the ring. Blake's interest was only half the reason I enrolled him for boxing lessons; my appreciation of hot, fit men was the other.

I shuffled onward, weighed down with bags of fruit I'd bought from the nearby Roman Road market. Salt trickles of perspiration made me blink. I breathed in the scent of masculinity, the familiar smell that never failed to arouse me. I'm a dirty old woman when it comes down to it.

The children's session had ended some time ago, so now the boxing hall was adults only. I wandered through the space, largely unseen as I edged past sinuous males lost in their physical pursuits. A row of tall men skipped rhythmically on the spot, their ropes making a steady *whoosh* as they twirled. I discreetly watched as the line of muscled bodies moved, noting how the different skin tones were laid out like a buffet before my hungry eyes. Several pairs of nipples jerked up and down, tantalizing treats I wanted to gobble up. The boxers were solid men, each one packed with muscle, but as they continued to skip, they truly looked weightless, as if they could simply take off and fly about the room if they wanted.

A hairy man did push-ups in a corner; my clitoris twitched at the sight of his piston contractions. I pictured myself beneath him as he moved up and down. I licked my lips; the mere thought was doing intense things to me.

I finally found my son in the back office. Blake sat with a tissue pressed to his bloody nose. His coach, Stefano, sat with him, one arm slung around his shoulder.

"What happened?" I held my son's face, tilting it to inspect the damage.

"Our little prize-fighter took on one of the older boys."
Stefano gave Blake a squeeze. My son jerked away, looking down
at the floor. "Only he didn't wait until he got in the ring."

"So what have you got to say for yourself?" I caught Blake's
chin, directed his face to mine.

"He said Great-Uncle Ray was never a fighter. He said his dad
could beat him up any day." The words came out in a flood.

"Go wait outside."

I sat down heavily next to Stefano. The coach reached over
and patted me on the knee. "Blake was actually quite impressive. He landed a good few blows before I managed to separate
the boys."

I sighed. "It's my uncle. He's a bit of a hero to Blake."

"Ah, yes," Stefano said with a wide smile. He leaned in
closer. "Quite a family you belong to. I never had a clue." When
he chuckled, his voice was rich, treacle sweet.

"Are you flattering me?"

"Is it working?" he asked with a raised eyebrow.

"Nah," I said, laughing.

"Your uncle is a bit of a hero to me as well. He was the
closest this club ever got to a world-class title holder."

"Until he got injured."

Stefano's eyes softened. "He's still a legend to some."

I took in the sight of the handsome coach. Growing up around
my uncle meant that my views on male physique were pretty
simple. I liked my men strong, lean and agile. Stefano ticked
all the right boxes. However he had none of the ego-tripping
personality that most boxers possessed. He didn't seem the type
to think that he was god's gift to women. That in itself would
have made him interesting, but it was all the optional extras
that made Stefano stand out. He had glossy collar-length hair
that I wanted to brush from his hazel eyes, broad lips that were

made for licking. If my eyes ventured lower I'd see his dark chest hair peeking out, a flat stomach and below that the uncharted territory of his crotch. I realized I was staring at it now.

I took a breath and composed myself before speaking once more. "It won't happen again. I'll have a talk with Blake."

Stefano patted me on the knee, a little higher than previously. Something flickered inside me; a little tremor in my belly. My thighs started to tingle from where his hand sat. I shifted on my chair, smiled.

"See you next week then?" I asked. It sounded like we were organizing a date instead of me simply collecting Blake as usual.

"I look forward to it."

The tingle grew stronger. My whole body thrummed with the urge to touch him. Somehow my mouth opened of its own accord. "Look, my uncle is staying with me this weekend. I'm sure he'd love to meet Blake's coach. Why don't you come over?"

Stefano's hazel eyes lit up. "That sounds great."

I caught sight of Blake as he stood outside the glass door. He looked at us with suspicion. That child was growing up too damn fast.

Uncle Ray wheeled himself into my kitchen that Saturday. I worked preparing dinner in the hot room. The air smelt of herbs and spices: rosemary I'd put on the potatoes, and fennel seeds I'd sprinkled on the pumpkin. However, none of the culinary aromas could distract me from the faint scent of Stefano's cologne as he stood close beside me.

"What are you doing in here?" Ray called out. "I've got more videos to show you yet."

"Help," Stefano whispered to me. "Your uncle's mad."

I stifled a laugh and continued to peel apples for the pie I was making.

"You can't watch all my other fights and miss this one!" Ray waved a DVD at us. "It's me in Germany, up against Eric Schmidt. He had the meanest right hook I've ever known."

Blake entered the room and pulled Stefano back to the lounge.

I joined the men as they sat on the sofa, eyes glued to the screen. I watched my uncle and the German as they moved about the ring. Their prowling steps were only disturbed by the heavy punches they threw. The cheer of the crowd seemed deafening, but with all the sights and sounds, I knew something was missing. I sat next to Stefano. His arm went instantly around my shoulder. I could smell his clean sweat mixed with the cologne he wore. This was what I needed. I reveled in the hard muscles that pressed against my shoulders; I leant against him to feel more. Uncle Ray looked at me; a sideways happy look, before he returned his attention to the recording.

When the bell rang for the end of round three, Ray flicked off the television. Blake made complaining noises, but my uncle shushed him.

"Come with me, boy. Let's make something really special to go with dinner." He wheeled himself out of the room, dragging Blake with him. "Did I ever tell you the time I cooked for the Lord Mayor of London?" My uncle's voice grew fainter as he moved to the kitchen.

Stefano pulled me closer without another word. He was strong where I was pliant, soft and yielding. When we kissed my hands went to his face. I hadn't noticed his long eyelashes before. It seemed such a feminine trait with all of his other masculine features, but it all fit. It was perfect. I brushed the hair from his eyes and then carded my fingers through his dark mane. He made a little sigh of pleasure. I took the opportunity to dot kisses over his lips, to suck them into my mouth as I kissed him again. I directed his hands to my breasts. I wanted him to touch me so much that I couldn't stand it. He pressed me with hard hands, rolled a nipple through the fabric of my dress. I couldn't help but moan quietly. All the stored power in his fists made me light-headed. I knew he could knock me out cold with just one well-aimed punch, but right now he was a lover, not a fighter. I clasped my own hands over Stefano's and felt the toughened knuckles against my palms. I'd lived all my life around a boxer, but I'd never been this close. I felt myself getting wetter by the second.

Stefano pulled back a little. "Much as I want you, your uncle scares me stiff." My hands swept down to his crotch at the mention of stiffness. I massaged the prominent bulge in his jeans; magic hands were a family trait I was grateful for. Stefano hissed. "After dinner, I promise I'll show you a good time."

"Okay."

We both wolfed down our meal, much to Ray's amusement.

Stefano practically jumped up from the table. He cracked his knuckles loudly. "Well, nice to meet you all, but I've got to run."

I stood too, kissed my uncle and my son on the cheek. I held Stefano's hand and led him outside to his car. I knew where I wanted to go.

When we arrived at the boxing club it was dark and empty. Ghostly shadows moved over the walls of the Victorian structure as we hurried inside. I took a deep breath; I caught the scent of perspiration, cleaning fluid and leather. It was an odd mix, but right then it was a complete aphrodisiac. The boxing ring came into view; the sight of it made the breath stutter in my throat.

"There." I pointed to the elevated platform. "Let's go there."

Stefano raised an eyebrow. "That's just a little bit kinky, but okay." He held up the ropes and let me clamber inside to the holy of holies.

Stefano approached me, fists raised; he danced around me, quick little steps as he gracefully bounced on the balls of his feet. He made short little jabs, coming closer and closer. I waited until he got into my range, and then I threw a punch of my own; he didn't see my right hook until it impacted on his jaw. I grew up around a boxer. I knew exactly how to use my fists.

"Are we going to fight or fuck?" I asked him sweetly.

Stefano looked dazed for a moment, and then he laughed out loud. I placed a hand on his shoulder and pressed him down to the mat. I straddled his hips and dry humped him until he groaned.

"I want to feel more of you," he breathed.

I stood and removed my knickers, while Stefano shed his clothes. I felt strong, aggressive and thoroughly sexy. I enjoyed the sight of Stefano's naked body, which was hairier than I had imagined. He was a strong man; every bit of him was hard, save for his furry balls that were crinkly soft as I licked them all over. I could smell his scent with every breath I took. I could taste him too, all seawater with a hint of smoke.

Stefano pulled me up so our faces met. He caught my wrists in his, and then he twisted his body in a sudden move so I toppled over to lie beneath him. Stefano was a solid weight on top of me. I wriggled, not in an attempt to get away, but because I wanted to feel more of his manly bulk. He shuffled lower, spreading my legs with his shoulders. He did nothing for a moment, except just gaze at my cunt. I started to feel a little self-conscious until I saw how the expression on his face had changed. Stefano looked hungry.

"Beautiful. You're beautiful," he said quietly. He pressed his face to my cunt. His mouth went everywhere, licking, biting. He devoured me. When I came, quietly gasping, I imagined I heard a crowd of sports fans cheering us on. Stefano moved back up to kiss me. I could taste myself on his tongue. The sensory bliss made my whole body start to throb once more. I directed Stefano's cock to my cunt. I inhaled his breath as he dropped a kiss to my mouth. He winked at me. "Ready for round two?" he asked.

"What did you have in mind?"

Stefano thrust inside me just once, and then he wriggled out.

"Hey, where are you going?" I felt empty without him. Stefano hauled me up, and then he directed me to one of the corner posts. "You have got to be kidding me!"

"You're the one with the boxing ring fetish. I just want to make sure you get the whole experience." He pressed me against the padded post, face-first. My hands gripped the ropes on either side. And then I felt Stefano's hard bulk against my back. He carefully spread my legs, angled my hips. He sank inside with a loud groan. I held on to the rope tighter as he gripped me with powerful arms. His graceful movements had vanished; hard urgent touches were all I felt. I wouldn't have it any other way. I might be left with a few bruises from our little tussle, but I would bear those marks with pride. Stefano's hips moved with speed. The angle of his cock made me hum with pleasure, plus my nipples rubbed against the post with a wonderful sensation. Stefano grunted once, twice, and then he stilled. I wondered why I'd never done it in a ring before, but then I thought of my uncle; this was his domain, and now I'd crossed over inside it. I wondered if he'd be glad or horrified to learn what Stefano and I had just done. I eased myself away from the post. I looked down to see a smear of come over the rubber surface. Maybe I'd keep this evening's fun from my uncle after all.

"Round three?" Stefano could barely stand, but he still beckoned me forward.

"Sweetheart, you wouldn't be able to walk if we went at it again."

"So do you admit defeat?"

I held up my hands in surrender. "You win. You are the greatest," I drawled. "Surely you are the heavyweight champion of the world." I started to giggle at that.

Stefano pulled the belt from his jeans. He held it up above his head and then proceeded to prance about the ring. "I am the champ!" he crooned.

I was still smiling when he took me home later. We'd gone another two rounds by then, but we decided to call it a draw. I was happy with the decision. Winning wasn't everything after all.

SACRED PLACES

Sophie Mouette

The drizzle of gray rain had driven the other tourists away from the monastery ruins growing out of the rugged Welsh landscape.

Kathleen stared at the altar—at what had once been an altar, but was now desecrated stone, robbed of its relics and smashed in half by Henry VIII's men centuries ago.

The words at the information plaque were a meaningless blur. It was so desolate here. Did anyone truly know what went on, day after day, night after night, if no outsiders were visiting?

She swore she could hear the monks chanting, low and melodious. Was the Latin in praise to God or some darker ritual?

A little way off, Ted picked his way through the shin-high ruined walls that delineated the monks' tiny cells. His scarlet rain slicker hood was up, his head down. The monks would all have been in brown or white, no way to distinguish one from the other when their hoods obscured their faces; even harder when it was dark, the only light from a flickering lamp or candle that tossed shadows across their mysterious features.

She'd never admitted it to anyone—not to former lovers, not to Ted, barely even to herself. There was kinky, and there was kinky, and for a former Catholic like herself, this was beyond even that.

Was that why she'd suggested they turn off here to see the ruined monastery in the Welsh mountains? It wasn't on their itinerary, but when she'd caught sight of the signpost, she'd blurted out the request.

Was her aim to indulge her deepest, darkest fantasy—or to receive penance for it?

And that was when the full-on shudder hit her, arousal clenching at her sex; her nipples and clit suddenly, almost painfully sensitive.

"Are you okay?" Ted had come up beside her. "You're cold; we should go."

"No, I'm fine," she said, and her voice betrayed her, a husky tremble that Ted had to recognize.

Either that, or the flush she knew had crept around her neck, and maybe the glassy look that had to be in her eyes.

"Kath?"

"I'm hearing voices," she managed. "Music."

He pointed to the side of the plaque on the wall of what had been the chapel, and she saw the little speaker grill. "They've got some Gregorian chant piped in. Pretty impressive when they don't even have a visitor's center."

She laughed nervously. "Of course." Of course she wasn't hallucinating. Of course Ted was the least monk-like creature she could imagine…yet in her current state of mind, she could envision his blue eyes brilliant and just barely visible under a woolen hood, his powerful body hinted at but not entirely disguised by his robe…although he'd have to lose his thick, shoulder-length dark hair, which would be a shame.

Bending close, he whispered in her ear, "I know that look. Kathleen Brigid Murphy, were you having dirty thoughts about monks?" He sounded stern, but she recognized unholy erotic glee when she heard it. The combination slew her every time.

Her cheeks flamed far more than she could blame on the spring breeze—and her cunt twitched, as hot as her face and, she realized, growing as wet as the mist on the breeze.

"No..." The denial was instinct. Some fantasies were just too weird, too shameful to confess, even to a husband who seemed utterly unshockable (and had a few weird fantasies of his own).

On the other hand, the remnants of Catholic guilt insisted honesty was the best policy, and so far it had been where Ted and sex were concerned. Every time she'd confessed a sexual fantasy, he'd gotten hard and hot and bothered and had done his best to enact it—usually with mind-blowing results.

"Okay, yes. I was thinking dirty things about monks. You happy now?" Merely whispering the words made her stomach lurch with a combination of nerves and arousal, made her breath come faster, made her lace bra feel stiff and scratchy against her insistent nipples.

"Tell me more."

She glanced around. The sun was starting to push through the streaked clouds, and any minute now a vanload of senior citizens could descend on the chapel ruins. Kathleen had lost a lot of her shyness since getting involved with Ted, but complete strangers, especially the elderly ones she imagined, didn't need to overhear her darker fantasies. "Later. Back at the B&B."

She should've known better than to try and negotiate. It always made things worse for her in the end.

So why was she suddenly wetter?

Ted smiled an evil smile full of dangerous promises. "Oh, no. You're telling me now. Right here." He backed her up into the chapel until her trembling thighs hit the ruined altar and she was forced to half sit on the broken stones.

She went unresisting. She wouldn't have been able to resist if she'd wanted to, and she didn't. When Ted decided to be all dominant and alpha like that, she turned to putty—and the fact that she'd been mentally tied to an altar and waiting to be ravished by anonymous monks made the puttying process that much faster.

He moved close against her, thigh to thigh, and slid his hands down her arms. His grip was loose, but he pinned her arms to her sides as effectively as if he'd used leather straps.

"Tell me," he repeated, and she knew better than to disobey a second time.

She told him how she felt the cold stone against her back, her ass, her legs. How coarse hemp rope—the rope of monks' belts—abraded her wrists and ankles where she was bound. She could smell beeswax and burning from the countless candles surrounding her, and myrrh and frankincense heavy in the air.

The candle wax, she knew, would be put to good use soon. She stifled a moan.

She was naked in the dark stone chapel, but that wasn't why she shivered. Fear and arousal mixed, a perfect, heady blend; and moisture was pooling between her spread-eagled thighs. At first, all she could hear was pigeons among the high, vaulted arches, cooing and rustling their wings. Then, distantly, came chanting, a solemn sound growing louder, and she shuddered right down to her clit.

Now the monks filed in, two by two in procession. Their chant didn't sound like any hymn she'd ever heard—this was pious, but laden with erotic promise. They were robed, hooded, anonymous, their faces lost in flickering shadow.

They surrounded her. Hands reached out...

Kathleen struggled for air, unable to keep talking. If Ted hadn't been standing so close, she thought she would have swayed and fallen.

"Well, well," Ted said, his low breath hot against her ear as he held her. "You do have a vivid little fantasy there, don't you? Tell me, do they pinch your nipples hard, like you like it? Do they drip wax on them? Do they reach between your thighs and tease your clit, laughing at how wet you are, at how close you get to coming before they pull away, denying you your release? Do they untie you and drape you face-first over the altar and whip your tender ass with birch branches, telling you how wicked you've been and how you need to be punished for your sins?"

His dirty litany not only built on her profane and secret confessions—it delved into her psyche and brought to light erotic details even she hadn't admitted to herself. The pressure had been growing inside her since they arrived. Now, with his obviously hard cock pressing against her sex and her mind racing with visions that aroused and shamed her in equal measure, she couldn't hold back.

And Ted knew it.

"Show the monks what a slut you are," he said, and she exploded, grinding against him even as she buried her face in his shoulder to muffle her screams.

When she stopped shaking, she grabbed his arm, tugging him back toward the rental car.

Ted tugged back, holding her in place. "Where do you think you're going?"

"Back to the car. I want to get you someplace more private."

Three older women with binoculars were heading up from the parking lot and Kathleen's still hungry body thought it was past time to get to the B&B and finish what they'd started.

"Not so fast. We haven't seen everything yet."

That was a change. She was usually the one saying that to Ted, who wasn't as fascinated with ruins as she was. And he never, ever put off a chance to have sex.

Unless, she realized with a sudden tug in her cunt, putting it off might make things more interesting later.

He put his hand on the back of her neck. His voice dropped to a throaty whisper that seemed to caress her clit as he said, "Take all the time you'd like here. I want you to have plenty of time to drink in the atmosphere and think about monks and the wickedness of your ways. A girl like you could ruin an entire monastery."

His voice, and the images it brought to mind of hooded figures and anonymous hands and vows of celibacy being thrown away like the day's trash, were enough to push Kathleen back to the trembling edge of orgasm.

Even without the sacrilegious pleasure of her fantasy, the monastery was worth closer exploration. As the sun came out, it became easier to imagine it intact, with robed brothers working in the herb garden, praying in the chapel, going about their day. At the same time, the contrast between bright sun and dark shadows made the ruins seem all that much more lonely and haunted, especially in the chapel, where the walls were just intact enough to give the feeling of an actual structure instead of rubble in the general outline of buildings. It was easy to imagine the chapel filling with ghostly monks at night—and who knew what depravities ghostly monks might practice?

The longer she spent there, the harder it was to separate herself from the fantasy.

And the few miles from the monastery to the B&B seemed like a trek across Asia.

* * *

They celebrated their arrival at the B&B with a round of fucking that made Kathleen fear for the antique bed—at least until she reached a point where she didn't give a damn about the bed anymore. It was hard, athletic, straightforward sex, with little connection to deviant monks, other than a few teasing sentences that got lost in the pursuit of more immediate pleasures, but Kathleen couldn't complain. Sharing the fantasy led to hot sex, and after all, that was what fantasies were for—even the ones that left you flushed and trembling with shame.

Ted was still flashing back to the interlude at the monastery himself, though, judging from some of the heated looks he gave her while they checked out the eleventh-century church in the town center, or the way he insisted they have a drink in the Tipsy Friar pub.

If Ted was still thinking about it, that meant it might crop up in some creative way when she least expected it. Would he enact some element of it or perhaps put her through "confession" and "penance" for having evil fantasies about holy men? Would he have her on her knees in front of him, admitting her wickedness in explicit detail? Torture her sins out of her like an inquisitor?

She shuddered with exquisite fear over her cider.

Unfortunately the cider conspired with several previous nights of more sex than sleep, and soon Kathleen was yawning over the last inch or so of her pint. "I need a nap," she confessed, taking her glasses off and rubbing her eyes. "Want to curl up with me?"

"I'll walk you back and tuck you in, but I need to pick up a few supplies in the shops."

She assumed he meant razors or deodorant, but by the time he returned with several shopping bags, she'd been asleep for a couple of hours and it was getting dark. He wasn't that into retail therapy, even in a place with a lot more shopping options than this town. Which meant he was up to something...but what?

From the secrecy and the smile, it had to be something erotic and exciting. And she was willing to bet that it had something to do with the taboo scene they'd woven in the monastery ruins. But what?

The conviction became a sexy certainty when he told her to wear a skirt and no panties to the country inn where they had dinner reservations. But nothing happened during dinner besides the usual flirting.

Comfortably full of venison pâté and salmon, pleasantly relaxed from pinot noir, lulled by Ted's hand on her knee, Kathleen took a few minutes to realize that Ted was driving farther out of town instead of back to the B&B.

"Where are we going?" she asked, although she had a wet, slippery, nervously excited feeling that she knew.

"Back to the monastery. It's past Compline on the Feast of Saint Bacchus and the good brothers are waiting for you."

He turned on the CD player and Gregorian chant poured out, spooky and stark and curiously sensual.

Arousal slammed into her like a fist. As they drove through the dark countryside, Kyrie Eleison soared around them. Ted's face was remote and he refused to answer her questions, saying all would be revealed in good time and then falling into silence so profound he might have been a holy statue on an altar— except for his fingers stroking the soft flesh of her inner thigh and occasionally teasing her labia and dipping into her cunt before retreating. By the time they arrived at the monastery she was moaning and keening through bitten lips, wanting to beg to come, yet, perversely, not wanting the erotic torment to end; curious and yet terrified to discover what her devious husband had in store for her.

The monastery ruins seemed deserted, not a car in the parking lot, not a sound other than the small bird-and-insect noises of night in the country.

But she could see candles burning in the chapel, just a few lights dancing in the darkness.

Kathleen's heart was pounding so hard she could hardly breathe, and her juices ran down her suddenly shaky thighs.

What had Ted done? He'd been with her for the past few hours. Would candles stay lit that long?

He couldn't have gotten other people in on this. Or could he?

She laughed with relief (or disappointment, but she didn't want to consider that) when they got into the chapel area and she saw no one else there.

The candles were the battery-operated kind and somehow—she couldn't begin to fathom how—Ted had procured a folding table, which he'd set up over the altar ruins and covered with a tarp. It was sweet, but it was kind of cheesy and...

Then he lifted his oversized sweatshirt and she saw the coarse rope he'd wrapped around his waist—the rope he was now unwinding with the obvious intent of binding her down—and something inside her broke. She no longer saw battery-operated candles or a modern folding table or even the stars twinkling between the empty flying buttresses.

Instead she saw an arched ceiling half lost in darkness and an altar draped with a richly embroidered purple cloth. She believed the candles were real and the melted wax painfully hot.

And she had no will to resist when Ted led her to the table, helped her onto it, and bound her ankles and wrists (dimly she knew the knots were loose, for quick escape if someone arrived, but she somehow really believed she was firmly tied down and utterly, completely, erotically helpless).

Gently, he took her glasses off and tucked them safely away,

then draped a cloth over her eyes. Not a full mask, but something with a loose weave.

"Can't have you seeing their faces," Ted said, his voice low.
"Can't have you telling. This way, you'll just have to guess how
many there are. How many touching you. How many watching
as you writhe and plead and come again and again."

Oh, dear god, he was right. Through the gauzy material
she could see the flickering candlelight, which cast shadows—
shadows that could be just shadows or could be robed men,
moving closer to stand in a ring around her, gazing at her half-
naked, spread-eagled, vulnerable form.

Then she heard a rustling followed by a striking match
and smelled beeswax, and her gut clenched, and if she could
have squeezed her thighs together she would have come right
then.

He'd already hiked her skirt up around her hips. Now he
unbuttoned her blouse and the front snap of her bra. Her already
aching nipples crinkled harder in the cool night air.

"Wicked girl," Ted said hoarsely. He tweaked both of
her nipples, twisting them to the point of glorious pain. She
arched her hips helplessly. "Fantasizing about men of the cloth.
Dreaming of them doing unspeakable things to you, all in the
name of earthly pleasures, pleasures of the flesh. Believing your
perverse sexual desires are sacred."

He released her throbbing nipples then, snaking a hand
down between her thighs. As he had in the car, he toyed with
her almost languidly, his fingers skidding through her wetness,
but without enough pressure to bring her to the release she so
desperately craved.

"Please," she managed. "Please."

"You have the audacity to beg?" he said. Whether the deep
voice was Ted or an anonymous monk, she didn't know. Didn't

care. The hazy covering over her eyes meant she could imagine it both ways.

Then, without warning, the first drop of wax hit her already tender nipple. The heat spread from her breast to her cunt, turning her body to molten lava. More searing wax, and she came, hard, muffling her own screams out of shame and fear, her shuddering body rattling the table beneath her.

Ted didn't let her rest or enjoy any after-orgasm languor. Before the final aftershocks had died away, he was already untying her, hauling her to her unsteady feet and turning her around, only to bind her facedown across the table.

She didn't know if she should be relieved that he hadn't managed to find a birch branch, but really, his broad hand on her naked ass was enough. He moved around her, smacking her with different hands and making it seem that the blows were coming from multiple men all around her. The shamed, excited part of her rode that feeling, believed the shadows conjured by her blurred vision until she could almost convince herself she could hear their voices, feel their woolen robes brushing her bare skin. The slaps were gunshots in the still night air, gunshots that ricocheted through her pussy, bringing her closer to the edge.

Ted (a monk?) moved around the table and faced her.

She actually worked one hand free so she could wrap her fingers around him, adding her hand to the ministrations of her mouth.

She was so close, almost desperate, but she knew she couldn't come like this, with her thighs spread wide and nothing touching her clit or driving into her. And the fact that her whole body screamed for release when the only release in sight was Ted's seemed perversely perfect.

Because there was more, more that she'd whispered to Ted in their B&B, her face flushed with shame and arousal. The monks tied her down and whipped her for having unholy sexual thoughts, for not being chaste. But when they saw how aroused she was—saw the wetness slicking her inner thighs, saw her hard, pouting nipples, saw her body arching and begging—then they succumbed to lust. The sight of her willing, wanton body was too much for them.

Because of her, they chose earthly pleasures—sexual release—over God Himself.

The thought of the monks coming for her and her alone, of them crying out God's name when they were really spurting their seed for her, on her, in her, was the crux of her fantasy.

Ted's hips jerked in a short, staccato rhythm, and she knew he was there. She tasted his first spurt on her tongue, and then he pulled back and splashed his come on her face, twitching and groaning.

She couldn't come like this, and yet she did, her cunt spasming as her orgasm wrenched through her, twisting her and releasing her.

This time she did scream, taking God's name in vain over and over again. Ted's cries joined with hers.

And as the echoes died away, they were together, at one with each other and with their private deity.

COUNTERPANE

Alison Tyler

T ake off the counterpane."

The boys were ahead of them. Not that the two couples were racing, but the blond stud was already on his back, head on the white-slipped pillow, slim hips arched. His dark-haired lover crouched between his thighs, licking that tender skin, working slowly to the blond's impressive hard-on.

Somehow Lia knew exactly how that would feel.

"Come on, baby. Help me with the counterpane." Ry was in a hurry to catch up. Lia could tell. Still, she turned to him, confused by his request.

"The *what*?"

"Bedspread," he said, his British accent stronger now that he was aroused. "Who knows how many people have shot their load onto those ugly watercolor flowers."

"How many do you think?" Lia asked as she helped him wrench back the heavy quilted comforter—abloom in gaudy burnt orange and lemon-yellow blossoms. She was looking at the boys again. For the first time in her life, she wished she had a cock—and she wished that the dark-haired Romeo was sucking her, right down to the root. She could almost feel his full lips on her skin—pretty, cupid-bow lips.

Ry gripped her chin and forced her to face him, his own lips bending into a half smile. "Slut." He elongated the word, really hitting the *l*. "That's your favorite part, isn't it? Thinking about all the other people who have fucked in this bed."

"*One* of my favorite parts." She pulled her chin out of his hand and stared back at the other couple, who didn't appear to mind in the least—the blond was tall and fine boned, the darker one well muscled, with tattoos scrolled over his skin. She'd hardly ever paused to notice gym rats before, but this guy did something to her. She watched the naked wrestling on the other bed—and she sighed out loud when the one with the chestnut hair hissed under his breath:

"*Roll over.*"

That was something Ry said to her, in just the same way:

"*Roll over. Show me that sweet fucking ass of yours.*"

Now, she watched as the top started to rim his lover. Fucking god. More than talking to Ry about who'd abused this hotel room before, she liked seeing what the two boys would do.

Her heart pounded at the way the brunet roughly pulled apart the blond's cheeks and licked in a tight circle around that tiny pink bud. She clenched her own thighs together. Ry had never done that to her. *Nobody* had. But she desperately wanted to own that experience, a tongue against her there. Wetness. Warmth. She thought that the sensation alone might make her come. Would it feel like Ry was suckling her clit? Would it make her feel like a boy?

The brunet didn't wait to see if rimming would make the blond come. He gripped a bottle of lube from the faux-walnut bedside table and poured a shivering handful between the lean man's taut cheeks. Lia moved forward. She wanted to be as close to the action as possible. She watched hungrily as the dark-haired boy slid one hand over his own rigid cock, lubing himself up, before pressing just the head against the blond's hole.

Right then, Ry grabbed her.

It was as if he'd been waiting for this exact moment—as if he knew what was going to happen next. His touch made Lia groan. All morning, she'd been thinking of this situation. While working in her sterile little cubicle downtown, she'd fantasized about what Ry had told her, where he'd wanted her to meet him for lunch.

Not to eat. But to fuck.

From outside, she could hear the noontime traffic. Through a crack in the window, she could smell the fried calamari sizzling in the kitchen of the downstairs café. But all that mattered to her were the people in this room.

Ry pushed her down on the bed and ripped her pleated violet skirt to her waist. She wasn't wearing panties—he'd told her not to when he'd instructed her to meet him at this hotel, on a Thursday at noon. This was the sort of thing Ry did from time to time: keeping her off guard, keeping her guessing.

The boys had already been going at it when she walked into the room, and she'd looked from them to Ry and back to them again, catching the grin on Ryland's face—seeing that he knew how excited she already was.

They didn't know the boys' names. But names didn't matter. All that mattered was watching them—she and Ry on one bed, the dynamic duo on another.

With her skirt pulled up to her ass, naked skin beneath, her pussy pressed hard against the crisp white sheets. She focused intently on the men—oh, the noises that they made. Those were almost as sexy to her as what they were doing. But then Ry did exactly what she'd fantasized about moments before. He slipped a pillow under her hips to raise her, parted the cheeks of her ass and pressed his tongue to her hole.

Jesus fucking Christ.

Why hadn't she let him do this before? He made one spiral and then another. She shut her eyes for a moment—because the wave of pleasure was almost too extreme—then opened her eyes and stared down at the forest-green carpeted floor, speckled with bits of lint. Ry slid one hand under her waist and touched her clit.

"Oh, baby. You're so wet. Look how wet you get when I lick you here."

Her cheeks burned as shame flooded through her. She couldn't speak. Ry's tongue between her cheeks turned up so many different emotions inside of her. Is that why she'd never let him do that before?

He licked her again, then moved back and pressed the ball of his thumb to her asshole. He didn't push it in; he simply rested his thumb against her. She waited. He didn't move. She waited another second. He was as still as she was. Finally, Lia couldn't stand the tease. She was the one to push back, to thrust back so that his thumb was inside of her and she was panting.

"You want it, don't you, you little slut?" he said. She loved when he talked to her like that. His accent made her feel exceptionally dirty. She had no idea why. Her eyes went back to the boys. The top was fucking the blond now at a rapid speed. She saw things she hadn't noticed at the start. The blond's nipples were pierced; his chest was waxed, smooth and bare. The brunet had a tattoo of an anchor on one shoulder, a '40s-style tattoo that made her want to trace the outline with her tongue.

"What are you thinking?" Ry asked, but she shook her head. He gripped on to her curls and pulled back hard. A shudder ran through her. His thumb was out of her ass now, and she could feel the head of his cock against her. Poised. Ready.

"What are you thinking, Lia?"

"That I'd like to lick him," she said. Her breath was coming faster now. "That I'd like to *be* him," she continued, unable to hold back as he pushed his cock into her. She wanted it all and all at once. She wanted to be the boy on top, licking the blond's hole, then fucking him. She wanted to be the blond, getting rimmed, getting fucked. She wanted to touch them, crawl into their bed, be a part of the game; turned inside out by the way they moved, the way they fucked.

There was a picture on the wall—a sailing print with a gold frame. The room had that antiseptic smell of cheap cleaning products, but beneath the scent was the odor of so many other guests who had romped here before.

But they hadn't been doing this, Lia thought. They hadn't been fucking in tandem like she and Ry and the duo on the other bed.

It wasn't a race—she knew that—but now the couples were moving beat for beat. Ryland was deep in her ass. The brunet was fucking the blond to the same exact rhythm. Their groans were a background melody.

Their very breathing was in synch.

When the movie ended, Lia came. Ry's cock was deep in her ass, and his fingertips stroked her clit, stretching out her orgasm. She sighed and pulled off him—feeling dirty and used and clean and set free. Ry reached for the remote control and turned off the porn channel. Through the bathroom door, she could see those familiar cheap white towels—nearly threadbare, too thin to be much use. She'd shower anyway, then head back to work—her ass sore, her body humming.

Ry said, "Next time, we'll take out an ad. Describe exactly what we want."

She looked at him, then at the dark box of the TV screen, and she nodded.

Because next time it was going to be for real.

WAISTED

Angela Caperton

R eady?" Monica asked with trepidation in her tone. "Last
one."

I gripped the mule post at the base of the foyer stairs and
nodded. My ribs protested under the pressure and my insides
creased beneath the stiff stays and beautiful, embroidered satin
brocade.

"There!" I felt the tug and zip as Monica finished tying
the bow at the base of the corset, the long remains of lacing
tucked up under the base crossings. With a sisterly pat on my
ass, she announced with some pride, "Done! Although I've no
earthly idea how you're going to breathe in that thing, much
less dance."

I released the post and took my first few careful steps to
the hall mirror. The lush, dusty lavender accented by scrolling
embroidery and black lace along the edges looked like something out of a dream. I felt every stiff stay that ran over my
ribs and stomach, and I suspected that if I wore the garment

too long, the thin padding beneath the front hooks and eyes
would dig into my skin. As I drew a restricted breath, the laces
at the back gripped like a silken steel cage, soft, moving just a
little as my inhalation tested the corset, but the bands remained
unfeeling, strict guards against excess.

I stared at myself, at the swell of my breasts cradled in black
lace and brocade, spared the total confinement of the rest of
the garment, then I let my gaze drift down to the artificially
narrowed waist and the feminine frill around my hips.

"I can't believe women used to wear those things all the
time," Monica said as she stood behind me, looking at my
reflection in the mirror.

I traced over the scrolling embroidery, my heart's rapid beat
more pronounced against my caged ribs. I nodded my agree-
ment.

"It is sexy, Kate. Graham's not going to know what hit him."

I shivered, smiling; fine, feminine bubbles rising in my blood.
Graham knew. Of course he knew. He had bought everything
I was to wear for the party, had insisted on outfitting me like
a queen for the occasion. He'd been so different about it too,
the damp dissatisfaction I had been feeling from him for weeks
completely absent when he'd told me where to go to pick up the
clothing. Even from across the country, his tone on the phone
had been apple crisp and edged with something I couldn't quite
place but had kindled a warm flame at the base of my spine
that heated each time he called with a new destination. First to
Lauren's Lingerie to collect the charcoal-black stockings he'd
ordered. Then three days later, it had been to Renau's Shoe
Boutique for the heels he'd picked out—all I needed to do was
try them on in my size. There had been a renewed spark in his
eyes when we'd had lunch two weeks ago and he told me my
dress awaited me at Vivian's Designs. Awaited me.

And it did—the beautiful, dark plum, strapless taffeta gown that swept the ground regally and showed off my shoulders and long neck. And waiting too was the corset with garter straps and a matching lavender and black thong.

I didn't want to think how much everything had cost Graham, and I struggled against a sour suspicion he'd gone through such effort out of an abundance of caution against my showing up for his company's charity bash dressed in an out-of-date consignment shop prom dress.

My fingers skimmed down the lines of the vertical stays. "I should finish getting dressed."

"Damn straight, sis. You've got less than an hour."

Monica waited at the base of the stairs like a mother seeing a daughter off on a date. She'd been that to me as well as a confidant as I picked up the soggy remains of my life. Without question, she took me in, gave me a shoulder when I needed it and left me my space in equal turns. She understood divorce and grief, and I know the shadows of Monica's life had helped me put order back into my own, post-Jeffrey. It had been Monica's husband Fredrick who introduced me to Graham on an early summer afternoon at the marina where Fredrick kept their boat. Graham's thirty-foot cabin cruiser bobbed in the slip beside Monica and Fredrick's, each mooring line neatly chalked off, the brass work shining like diamonds, the bumpers tied to the gunwale in precise knots. Graham's smile had fluttered my belly and while the conversation had been brief, it had been enough. He called the next day to ask if I'd like to go with him to a concert at the botanical gardens.

In short order, Graham burned away the confusion and guilt I'd all but tattooed to my psyche, and we'd dated steadily for eight months and enjoyed some great sex. He'd even taken me to New York for a long weekend, but for the last three months, he seemed to be pulling away, distracted, and even in bed he seemed vaguely absent. His travel schedule had become insane, and I chalked it up to stress, but I struggled to identify the source, or how I might help.

And now, with this party, and his new attitude—I had a sense of a threshold, but of what sort, I could not guess.

He'd hired a limo for the night, a tasteful black sedan with a quiet driver, and when it arrived he handed me into the butter-soft leather seats. I couldn't stop smiling as I gathered the skirt of the dress around me. Graham's eyes had glowed when he saw me at door, and they hadn't stopped.

He got into the car on the other side and immediately took my hand, bringing it to his lips for a tender kiss.

"I knew you would look spectacular," he said, a small, secret smile on his face. He traced a single knuckle down the exposed line of my neck.

"It's the most beautiful thing I've ever worn, Graham: the dress, the corset, everything," I practically cooed. "I feel completely feminine, and I love it."

He turned from me, looking past the driver to the road. "What does it mean to feel feminine?"

The question hung a moment between us. "That's a loaded question."

"What does it mean to you?"

"It's not a static feeling, and I suspect different women have different definitions. For me, right now, it feels like a mix of potential and chance, sexual power and mystery. Flirtation and seduction, exuberance, grace, the thrill of being adored and wanted. It's magic." I squeezed his hand lightly and he turned back to me, his smile quirking at the corners.

"Is that all?"

I laughed and he raised my hand to his lips again, lightly raking his teeth over one knuckle.

He released my hand and turned back to the road.

"Kate, remove your panties."

At first, all I could do was blink, my throat suddenly dry, the inevitable question caught in the constriction of the corset.

"What?"

The quiet hum of the limo swirled around us for several rapid heartbeats. Graham turned to me, unsmiling, but with that same spark in his eyes that he'd shown at lunch two weeks ago.

An odd tickle teased the base of my stomach, whipping my pulse into an uneasy staccato. Slow heat spread over my hips and freed the first slick of arousal in my pussy.

I glanced at the back of the driver's head, at the rearview mirror, hoping he hadn't heard Graham, hoping his forehead would be all I saw in the mirror as I started to slide the dress up my legs, then wickedly hoping he had excellent hearing and eyes in the back of his head.

My fingers fumbled as I shifted a little and unsnapped the garters from my stockings, then slipped the delicate thong over my ass, exposing my damp pussy to the suddenly warm air in the limousine. I looked over at Graham, but he didn't watch me, instead looking out the front windshield, his face impassive, his eyes unreadable. I quickly fixed the garters to my stockings, then worked the thong down my legs, the air pushed almost violently from my diaphragm as I bent to step out of it.

"Leave them on the floor," Graham said with a calm tone he might have used to order a drink.

What paltry breath I had in my lungs froze, my cheek almost to my knees as I held the delicate material in my fingers; I felt a stab of...of...of what? What was the sharp ache clenching my hand but rushing my heart? I released my grip and the thong remained on the impeccably clean carpet of the car, evidence of my complicity. I sat back up, my lungs greedily cooling with the measured inhalation the corset allowed me. I sat back against the seat and settled the skirt around my legs.

My ankles burned from the heat of the thong between them.

The creak of the leather seats and the rustle of the taffeta were the only sounds for several moments. Graham didn't look at me, and after my heart began to slow, I tried to relax.

Tried to relax even as I leaked between my uncovered pussy lips.

"How do you feel, Kate?" Graham asked quietly. He looked at me again with the barest hint of a smile.

The question slapped my nerves and my heart skipped to fourth gear. My cheeks burned as much as my ass did against the stiff taffeta, and more shivers of wet pleasure bloomed in between my legs.

"I feel...I don't know how to say. I...I feel like I'm walking in a labyrinth."

"Are you frightened?"

Static pressed against my eardrums, but his voice pierced through precisely. The pounding in my wrists and at my throat thudded like the hammer fall of a sculptor. "Yes, some, but...I like it."

He smiled, and it seemed genuine if controlled, the slight curve of his lips more true than any other expression I had ever seen on his face.

The limousine stopped at the opulent hall where Graham's company held their charity event every year. I didn't see the limo driver as he handed me out of the car; the image of the lavender thong on the floorboard exposed for all to see burned my vision. When Graham placed his hand on the small of my back, the center of his palm crossed the valley of the corset laces and my skin under the material seemed to swell, soft and sweet like a marshmallow browned by a careful flame.

My ears rang with names and polite conversation as Graham introduced me to executives and dignitaries. A wonderful nervous simmer in my belly fed warmth to my skin, my mouth, but it wasn't born of swirling music or the stream of people around me; it bloomed from Graham's hand, the slightest pressure of his fingers against the back of the dress, the pad tracing imperceptibly to anyone but me the laces over my spine. A lush tingle ran up the back of my neck, the upswept hair masking a blush of arousal that fed the growing wetness in my pussy.

I found refuge in the cage of the corset, as if the silky material and stiff stays kept my growing desire in check. We mingled, we danced, we sat and dined, and Graham's hand possessed me, held me to him like a leash, the small strokes against the crisscrossed laces as powerful as a kiss. I floated through the night nearly blind to everything except him, each stingy breath bringing me one more ache closer to knowing him. After hours of socializing, when finally Graham whispered in my ear, the bolt of lust that blasted through me nearly emerged in a moan.

"It's time to go."

I hardly saw the lights, barely heard the drone of cars on the road, almost missed the stop and start of the limousine—every sense, every nerve ending collected under Graham's still, hot hand where it rested on my thigh. My heart pounded between the tight hooks of the corset and the desire to beg, to plead for his fingers to grace the corset strings again nearly overwhelmed me. I had had one glass of wine at the reception and was more intoxicated than I had ever been in my life. When I'd stepped into the limo, my thong was still on the floor, a brand of shame and freedom born of the very same release. The crumpled silky fabric lay hot between my feet. I struggled not to crawl into

Graham's lap, while I fought to obey the calm, steady palm on my thigh. My blood and my pussy fueled both a hungry arousal and a hard, urgent desire to rebel, to destroy without reason—twins of fire I never knew lurked within me.

He didn't say a word during the ride, and upon our arrival, only opened the front door of his house, not even glancing back at me, and walked straight up the stairs toward his room. I followed without question and at the top, the fleeting question passed, should I close the door?

I walked to his bedroom, the dress suddenly a thousand pounds, the corset cold without the heat source of Graham's hand. I stood at the threshold, acutely aware that passing beyond the door would change everything for me, for him. I wanted the cool calm of a deep breath, but the corset denied me that simple sanctuary. Everything about this moment would be deliberate, nothing left to physiology or chance. I step into his room, I step into his hold.

His control.

Blood rhythmically beat against the back of my eyes as he removed his cuff links, unbuttoned his shirt. He didn't look at me, but he knew I was there, wavering, and although his expression never changed, I knew to linger too long between worlds would disappoint him.

Graham wanted decisiveness—in action, in thought, in purpose.

Giddy with an oddly born sense of power, I stepped into his room and went to his side, wanting with all my heart to touch him but not daring, afraid beyond reason my clumsy attempt would melt the magic like fire on wax. His body heat stroked my skin in elusive waves as he stripped down to nothing within inches of me. He never acknowledged me, never looked at me, just continued his routine as if I were a ghost, a pesky shadow on the mirror above his bureau, and I held back again and again the conditioned bleat that would demand his acknowledgment.

This wasn't about me, and yet it was—about me and about him. Some alert corner of my brain processed, filtered, edited, condensed every moment of the last few weeks, rendering down action, reaction, conversation and sensation into the thick, sweet essence of pilgrimage.

Somehow, the corset pointedly, precisely forced me to think about everything—including a fought-for full breath.

He stood before me, toned and sleek, his skin marked by tan lines and the long scar on his right shoulder, memento of a car accident long before I knew him. His cock jumped a little as it grew erect under my gaze, and I smiled, a slow, spreading blush that percolated through my entire body. He looked at me finally and the punch of his gaze almost staggered me: penetrating black eyes, confident, almost cold, except for the fire I saw there. He lusted, he wanted, and he wanted me.

But not just my body, I could see that. His body couldn't mask his desire, but in that first braising appraisal, I knew this wasn't just about fucking, and with everything that had happened that evening, I knew I wanted what he did—even as I acknowledged my shaky concept as to what that want was.

He reached for me, taking me at the waist, his strong hands implacable. He studied me—shoulders, neck, the curve of my breasts above the bodice of the dress—his hands starting a slow kneading, tightening then loosening around my stomach, the rhythm deliberate as he continued his examination of my hands, my arms, my shoulders. My body, barely under my control throughout the night, shocked me with a punch of primal arousal, the pulse between my legs a perfect cadence with my racing heart. His cock jumped against the taffeta, a shining, dark smear marking me as his. He released my waist and ran his hand up the side, unzipping the dress, then pulling it away. He lifted me out of the pool of fabric, setting me on the thick carpet beside his bed. I stood still, empowered by the controlled hunger I saw in him. He traced along the bodice of the corset even as his other hand teased my thigh where my garter held the stocking. I swallowed my fear and reached up to his cheek, a light press of flesh to flesh that nearly overwhelmed me. His hand left my thigh and he slid his fingers between the soaked curls of my pussy.

Feral and low, his whisper raked like a whip. "Take off your shoes." His fingers circled my clit as I slipped out of the heels. I wanted to grind against his hand, to spear myself on his cock, but he took his fingers out of me and raised them to my lips, smearing my own juices over them. The gleam in his eyes was demonically wicked. I flicked my tongue out, cleaning the tip of his index finger before he put his hands on my shoulders and exuded pressure, undeniably wanting me on my knees. God, yes! I'd show him how much I wanted him; my mouth watered at the thought of sucking him dry.

But as I went down on the handmade silk rug, he deftly stepped behind me, denying me the taste of him, the joy of his cock inside my mouth. He ran his hands over my shoulder blades, tracing the edges of the corset, then plucked at the crossed lacing at the center of my back and, as if the strings were wires connected to my pussy, the sensation electrified me. He ran both his hands over my ass, then slid one up to my pussy again, testing me, stroking me, driving me crazy. My breath puffed in short, starved bursts, the corset still firmly in place. The slightest bit of relief came when he pulled at the excess lacings where Monica had tucked them at the base of my back. I felt the tickle of him untying me. I ran my hands over the front, ready to spring myself by opening the front hooks and eyes.

"No," Graham said without color or bite.

I forced my hands to my sides, my breath shivering in and out as anticipation grew in me. One of Graham's hands spanned between my shoulder blades as he pressed me down to my hands. "Down. All the way."

Prone. Vulnerable. Memory flared a hiccup of panic in my throat, my body going rigid as I took possession of the fear. I lay on the thick rug, willing my muscles to relax. Graham's hands stroked and teased the back of my neck, the span of my shoulders, turning me into a puddle of want. I found myself entranced, moving like a charmed snake, supple shrugs and swaying hips under the mystery of his touch.

My brain tried to reason, tried to assess the surrender, but the thick thud of my heart, the roaring rips of swelling desire in my ears smashed reason to bits. Graham's hands ran down the back of my arms and closed around my wrists, pulling with care to cross them at the crest of my buttocks.

I was so hot, so utterly alive, every nerve overtaxed with the erotic pop of his strokes, it didn't register at first. He used the lace ends to tie me, skillfully binding my wrists together at the small of my back, my captivity nearly complete.

He moved between my legs and lifted my hips, forcing me onto my knees. I groaned out a breath, Graham's intention feverishly clear. I wished I could see my wrists, the laces of the corset branding my skin in ribbons of fire that frightened and electrified me. He slid a hand over my ass, his fingers drenched in evidence. Expertly, he found my clit, giving it a squeeze that asserted control and I moaned, the sound involuntary but unstoppable. I tried to catch my breath but the corset denied me the calming coolness of full lungs.

And as I blurted out the abbreviated breath, my ribs and diaphragm strained against the increased constriction of the corset. Graham, with one hand teasing my clit, pulled against the lacings with the other, tightening, forcing the corset tighter, harder, encasing my torso in brocade and rigid metal, unyielding cotton and eyes slicing space. The sound that escaped my throat had no force, the air conservative and stingy. His relentless fingers continued to stroke and pluck at my clit, and as my head spun with the enormity of what I was doing, what he was doing, my pussy boiled with truth, flowed over his hand, wept for completion.

I barely felt his cock at the gate, but as he pushed into me, hard, direct, adjusting the angle of my hips, the corset tight around me, my charged senses registered every millimeter of his penetration.

I cried, my lungs hungry for more air. The tender ducts of my eyes forced tears; forced the joyful, fearful, amazed celebration of his finally fucking me out of my body, acknowledging the wonder.

He groaned. I heard it and felt the edge of orgasm rush forward. His cock began a fast, hard pistoning; the solid invasion, the complete sense of surrender bucked against my need for him, my longing; my shredded naïve notions of love replaced with something I didn't yet understand, didn't fully comprehend, but that I felt being forged in the white hot heat in my aching chest, under the strong pounding of my heart and his cock.

The edge didn't loom, and it wasn't emblazoned in white light. It was red, alive, angry and molten—lava sliding out of a crack in the earth to burn away the old and build new, fresh land.

My pussy clenched, the saliva in my mouth pooled on the carpet—and behind me, fucking me, possessing me, Graham's panting breath finished me. I came hard, wave after wave of obliterating pleasure pulsing from my cunt, blasting through the cage around my body and tearing the scream from me in ragged, joyful chords.

He didn't stop, his cock still thrusting, piercing, binding me to him as the orgasm rocked through me, and as I half feared the pain of wasted flesh abused, he thrust harder, deeper, splitting my pussy.

Abruptly, he released the laces, and the corset, victim to physics, loosened, freeing me, gripping me just barely less than it had all evening, but my pussy, my ribs, my lungs, opened.

Golden light, flashing harmonies, the instinctual gasp of the first full breath I'd taken all night obliterated every nerve, every instinct, every reservation and thought. I shuddered, clenched, gasped and came again, savoring a final slap on my ass as Graham growled and came, filling me with his semen, searing me with the brand of ownership.

He collapsed over me and together we sank to the carpet. His ragged breath echoed mine as I savored every fiber of the rug, every inch of his warmth, the slow slide of his spent cock out of me, the cool wetness as I dripped on silk.

One of the stays of the corset dug into the flesh beneath my breast and I giggled, joyful, content and embracing the unknown itinerary of this journey Graham had started me on.

He kissed the back of my neck, tender, loving, and a full body shiver pebbled my skin and hugged my waist where the stays of the corset rested.

I closed my eyes, content to be pinned.

Pinned, bound, caged within stays and ribs, exhausted and totally, completely happy for the first time in my life.

So sweetly spent. So completely and delightfully waisted.

UNDERPANTS

K. D. Grace

Don't get dressed," Dan whispers into the phone. He's just come, and I can hear the drowsiness creeping into his voice. "I want to dress you." His words soften like warm butter. "I dream of dressing you."

My fingers are still curled over my pubis, slick and warm from my orgasm. I smile into my pillow where the phone is cradled against my ear. "I'm in bed. I won't need dressing until morning."

"I mean when I get there tomorrow night. Let me dress you. I have a surprise for you," he adds, just in case I might need convincing.

I don't.

Dan's full of surprises. That's why I still fuck him. Knowing that I'm the other woman makes the sex more exciting. Maybe it's knowing he doesn't want me to settle down and have his children.

I don't ask how he manages our one evening a week. I don't

care. I don't even know his partner's name. I get my weekly shag and just enough risky phone sex to turn me all Pavlovian every time my mobile goes off.

The next evening I indulge in a candlelit bath with lots of bubbles. I lie back with my eyes closed and masturbate. When I answer the door, I'm primed and ready, wrapped in a blue silk robe, hair and makeup perfect. I go all tingly as I imagine being wide-eyed and naïve, needing the help of someone older and wiser to dress me properly for a night out in London. I feel wickedly innocent standing before Dan, clutching the robe around me demurely.

He kisses me, eating my mouth like it's chocolate. "Traffic's awful," he says, pulling away enough to trace the lapel of my robe down between my breasts to where it crosses under the knotted sash. His eyes are as hungry as his mouth, following the trail of his hand.

It's then I notice the package, about the size of a thin book. It's wrapped in gold paper, tied with a red ribbon and a single rose. I reach for it, but he pulls it back offering me a teasing smile. "When I decide you're ready for it, you'll get it."

He takes my hand and leads me into my bedroom, tugging open my lingerie drawers and running thick fingers over neatly folded bras and thongs. Then he shakes his head and shoves the drawers shut. "Not right for tonight."

I feel pleased. He knows I love sexy lingerie. Surely that's what's in the package. He throws open the closet door and paws through my clothes. "I want something soft and revealing." He glances over at me. "I want easy access to disguise a multitude of indiscretions." His gaze locks on my crotch, and I feel breathless.

"How about this?" He pulls out my favorite dress, black silk and chiffon with a short flip skirt. The top shows more cleavage than anything I own. When I reach for the drawer with the appropriate lingerie, he pushes my hand away. "I'm dressing you, remember?"

"But—"

"Shh." With one hand, he unties the robe and shoves it off my shoulders. Then he pulls the dress from the hanger and motions for me to raise my arms.

When he slides it over my head, I'm sputtering about the proper bra and thong, certain men don't know about these things, but he isn't listening. He pinches my nipples through the dress until they're distended and sensitive, and even the touch of silk makes them ache.

"Perfect," he says. His voice has gone rough, and when he takes off his jacket, like he's getting down to serious business, I can see the press of his penis distorting Armani trousers.

He rummages in the top drawer beneath the thongs and knickers and finds black suspenders, old ones, ones I seldom wear. I'm starting to wonder what he has in mind. Then he lifts the dress until I can see my bottom reflected pink and freshly scrubbed in the mirror behind me. He sees it too and takes his time to admire it, turning me this way and that, cupping me, spreading me just enough for a glimpse of what I know he wants.

When the suspenders are secure, he sits me on the bed and kneels between my legs. Slowly he teases sheer black stockings up my thigh, pausing to run his tongue over the arches of my feet and kiss me on the spot where he attaches the stockings to the suspenders. I feel his hair, still damp from the weather, brush against my mons, and my labia shiver and grasp. "There," he sighs, when he's done.

I don't care about the restaurant anymore. I want him now. But he ignores my efforts to wriggle closer. He helps me into black stiletto sling-backs that have *fuck me* written all over them. Those, I knew he would choose. They're his favorites.

"Almost ready." He's breathing harder now, but so am I. I feel half-naked and naughtier somehow without the appropriate underpinnings. He's taking me to some Italian trattoria I've never heard of. He says he likes the atmosphere. That usually means a place dark and intimate enough that the meal is a yummy grope fest, and I'm the main course.

I giggle and open my legs. "What? No knickers?"

"Of course knickers. I'm not taking you out dressed improperly." He sounds proprietary, as though my virtue is his to protect, and I feel even naughtier. He hands me the gold-wrapped box. While I shred the wrapping, he takes the rose and brushes the petals up the length of me. The room is awash in the scent of rose and pussy.

For a second, I think he's having a laugh. But he waits expectantly, all wicked smiles, as I unfurl the huge pair of white cotton knickers that my nan would have found prudish. I'm thinking surely there must be a sexy lace thong underneath, or maybe hidden inside.

There isn't.

"You're joking. Right?"

"I'm serious." He lays the rose aside and takes the knickers from me. He slips my stiletto clad feet through the giant leg holes, then shimmies them up my thighs. "Lift your bottom for me," he says. "There we go. That's my girl."

I'm too shocked to argue. He drags them up over my bum, and they keep going until they're scant centimeters beneath my breasts.

"You're joking," I repeat.

He's practically on top of me in his monumental struggle with the big knickers, enjoying the experience a lot more than

I am. His cock is digging enthusiastically into my thigh as he presses closer. "I promise it'll be good." Then he slides his hand over the acres of white cotton onto my mound. "I want to keep you all safe and tucked away just for me."

I think he's going to pull the crotch aside and finger-fuck me. Instead, he grabs the whole gusset and gives it a hard yank.

I yelp in surprise as his efforts nearly slide my bottom off the bed. Then I watch in fascination as he ties the large crotch into a tight, compact knot, pulling the gaping legs of the knickers down tight around my thighs as he tugs and shapes. With one hand, he holds my labia open and with the other he wriggles the wad of scrunched fabric up snug between my lips, like he does with his penis sometimes when he's teasing me. He pushes and shoves and adjusts until I can just clench my muscles around it.

"There," he grunts, pulling away and offering me a hand to stand. "That's perfect."

As I struggle up from the bed against the press of the knot, he glances at his watch. "Come on. We don't want to be late."

The taxi is waiting, and amid breathless curses and protests, I follow Dan down the steps frantically clenching the knot that, I'm sure, is the only thing keeping the big underpants from dropping embarrassingly around my fuck-me shoes.

In the taxi, he puts his arm around my shoulders and slides his hand into my dress, his eyes daring the taxi driver to enjoy the view. He guides my palm under the edge of his jacket to his hard cock. As I grope, I catch the flutter of his eyelids before he pushes my hand away. He's teasing himself as much as he's teasing me.

He strokes my nipples into hard little bullets, and the knot of underpants pressing into me becomes a slippery dildo. With the vibration of the car beneath me, I'm practically fucking cotton.

I'm breathing hard, about to come, when the taxi stops, and Dan pays the driver.

I can barely walk as the waiter seats us, and for one horrified moment I think I'm going to come in the middle of the restaurant and lose my grip.

The chairs are hard wood, making the knot feel like a fist each time I lean forward in my seat. Dan orders expensive champagne and antipasto, and the waiter gabbles on about specials. But I'm thinking about the big knickers, not sure if I want them off or further on.

I excuse myself to go to the ladies', and as Dan stands to pull out my chair, he whispers close to my ear. "Don't be long, or I'll think you're up to something." He gives my nipple a pinch. I gasp and clench and hurry off to the loo.

The ladies' room is only a one-seater with no stalls, and I've barely gotten my hand under my skirt when there's an urgent knock on the door. Some poor woman may be waiting in extreme discomfort, and here's me playing with myself. I sigh and give the toilet an unnecessary flush before I open the door, and Dan pushes his way in, shoving the lock tight behind him. He jerks my hand to his nose and sniffs. "You were playing with your knickers." It isn't a question.

He forces me forward over the sink, bending me until the reflection of my tits bounces in the mirror. Behind me, he lifts my skirt, and I yelp in surprise as the first smack of his hand comes down onto my white-knickered bottom. "I get to dress you." *Smack.* "I get to play with you." *Smack, smack.* "My rules," he puffs in my ear.

"You didn't say anything about rules," I growl. "And besides, if I don't do something these damn things will be down around my—" I suck air as his hand comes down again on my bottom. I've never contemplated the sound of a hard smack against heavy cotton knickers before, and I don't contemplate long. Dan turns on the cold water and shoves his hand under it. Then he thrusts a wet finger against my anus and wriggles and pokes. In my already desperate state, it takes about two seconds for me to orgasm. With my back hole gripping his cotton-clad finger, I nearly bounce him across the ladies' room in my spasms.

He steps back and admires his handiwork. "Feel better? I daresay you won't lose your panties now." He takes my hand. "Pasta's getting cold."

Wobbly legged, I follow him back to the table in an endorphin haze, sitting very carefully with both my holes full of cotton.

Through the entire four-course meal, I think only of the big cotton knickers and what they do to me each time I move. And Dan, that horny bastard, knows exactly what they're doing to me. He also knows that I know he's sitting there with a raging hard-on.

The taxi ride home is interminable. He doesn't touch me this time. He doesn't dare. When we arrive, he hands the taxi driver a wad of bills and drags me upstairs. We're barely inside before he's shoving me toward the bedroom, shedding his clothes as he goes. By the time he pushes me onto the mattress, he has kicked off his shoes and stumbled out of trousers and boxers.

I get a brief view of his cock before he's on top of me, nuzzling into my cleavage, shoving lace and chiffon up until he can finger the elastic top of the granny panties. Then, with a yank that feels like he'll jerk me inside out, he pulls the knickers down, and I scream—not because it hurts, though it does. I scream because I'm in convulsions from the orgasm he's yanked out of me along with the knickers.

He pulls them off me and shoves them in my face. For a frightening moment, I think he's going to gag me with the same knot that's filled my pussy, and for an even more frightening moment I think I might not actually mind if he does.

But he doesn't.

He pulls them to his face and snuffles and suckles. "I'm mad for your scent," he groans. "You're all I could smell all evening."

Then he grabs my wrists, both in one large hand, and binds them to the headboard with the knickers, the knot pressing into my pulse points, a reminder of just how unforgiving cotton can be.

I watch wide-eyed, helpless as he runs curious fingers over my raw gash that now feels agonizingly empty without the knot. It grasps at him, and I squirm and whimper trying to force myself toward his erection.

"A little restraint suits you." He slides two fingers into me and chuckles as I hump them. "Maybe I've given you free rein too long." He bends and gives my nipple a tug between his teeth, and I buck and growl, ready to rip his throat out if he doesn't give me what I need.

But I'm not the only one who's been restrained all evening, and he shoves into me with such force that I bump my head against the headboard and curse. I shove back so hard I hear his joints pop. He vise-grips my arse and thrusts deeper. I wrap my legs around him and dig my heels in like he's a horse, and I'm the jockey. He doesn't make it last, and I don't want him to. All evening has been foreplay, and I can't wait any longer. I come first, then he rips the bindings from my wrists and grunts his ejaculation into the crumpled cotton.

In the morning, he stuffs the big underpants back into the box he brought them in.

"You're taking away my gift," I joke.

"It's not your gift," he says, dropping a kiss on my lips. "It's my gift to me."

"Make sure you hide them where your partner can't find them," I tease.

He tucks the box inside his jacket and studies me for a long moment, then his mouth curls in a half smile. "There is no partner, darling. I thought you'd have figured that out by now." Then he hurries off to catch the taxi waiting outside.

RED

Piper Morgan

B ode looked at her expectantly.

"That's it? That's your fantasy?"

He crossed his arms and sighed. "That is exactly why I didn't tell you."

"What?"

"You're making fun of it."

Amelia smiled as she walked over to him and sat on his lap. Kissing the top of his head, she wrapped her arms around his shoulders, his bare skin warm to her touch. "I'm sorry, Bode; I didn't mean it that way. It's just the way you fought tooth and nail about telling me, I thought it'd be really weird. Or gross."

His face brightened like a child seeing a table full of birthday gifts. "Really? Does that mean you'll do it?"

"Of course."

Bode squeezed her small waist and planted a huge kiss on her full lips. "I love you, Amelia. This is why you're the greatest."

She kissed his neck and ran her tongue up to his ear, finally sucking his earlobe. "I know," she whispered, letting her warm breath tickle the wet trail her tongue left behind.

Goose bumps rose all over Bode's wide chest. He slipped his warm, plump tongue in Amelia's mouth as he lifted her and took her over to the couch.

Bode was typing up his final reports when his cell phone beeped. He flipped it open and smirked. Amelia had sent him a picture of her long legs, barely covered in black fishnet stockings, with her text: *Everything's set for this weekend. Leave work as soon as you can. I'm ready...grrr.*

On my way, he texted back.

Bode quickly finished his reports, sent them and shut down his computer. He grabbed his briefcase and quickly walked out of his office. "Bonnie, I'm going out of town for the weekend. See you on Monday."

"But, sir..."

"Cancel everything," he called back as the elevator door closed.

Bode loosened his tie as he rushed up the porch steps two at a time. He unlocked the door and quickly slammed it shut behind him, literally dropping everything when he saw Amelia. Standing at the base of the stairs, she wore only the fishnets, clunky-heeled black boots and a short, red velvet cape, her creamy white skin beautiful, almost glowing, against the dark color.

"Hi, sexy." Amelia winked and opened the clasp on the cape. It fell to a crumpled heap at her feet on the hardwood floor.

Bode rushed to her, wrapping his arms around her waist and pulling her into him, her full breasts pressed against his hard chest. Through the thin fabric of his shirt, he could feel that her tiny nipples were erect, ready to be licked. He kissed her hard as his hands worked their way down her hips, finally cupping her round ass. He gave a small squeeze as she gripped his biceps.

Amelia pulled away from his moist lips. "I thought this was for tomorrow."

"No reason we can't have some fun before we get to the cabin." He raised his eyebrows and smirked before dipping down to kiss her jawline.

Amelia watched the trees in various shades of green all around them, as Bode slowly drove down the steep dirt drive. At the bottom of the driveway was a tiny lake surrounded by several weeping willows. The scene was so peaceful and beautiful.

She smiled. "We're having sex over there sometime this weekend."

Bode hit the brakes, the car sliding a little in the gravel. He followed the direction her finger pointed and laughed. "Fine by me, Amelia. We can have sex wherever you want." He let off the brakes and continued to the side of the small cabin.

He parked the car, helped Amelia out and grabbed the suitcase from the backseat as she unlocked the front door. She pulled open the shades to let in the bright morning sun.

The living room had a blue and white gingham love seat, a solid wood coffee table and a midnight-blue area rug in front of the fireplace. It opened up to the tiny kitchen where a small square table and two wooden chairs sat in the corner. A bathroom was off the kitchen.

Amelia walked up the spiral staircase followed by Bode. The only thing in the loft bedroom was a dresser with an oval mirror and a king-size bed covered by a patchwork quilt. He put the suitcase on the floor and went back downstairs. They walked out the back door and stood on the porch, overlooking the sea of trees, before Amelia looked to her right.

She smiled as she lifted the cover off the hot tub and put her fingertips in the warm, bubbling water. "This will be fun too."

Bode wrapped his arms around her waist and kissed her shoulder. Amelia moved her long auburn hair and leaned into him as he kissed her slender neck. He started fondling her breasts before she stopped him and turned to face him.

"Not yet."

His shoulders sunk and his smile faded.

Amelia smiled. "Very soon, love. You have a fantasy we need to get ready for." She grabbed his hand and led him back inside, up to the bedroom. "Sit down and close your eyes." She watched him go over and lay down on the bed. "Are they closed?" Amelia went to the side of the bed and started unbuttoning his shirt. Bode started to open his dark blue eyes. She quickly straddled his chest and bent down, planting light kisses on his eyelids. "Keep them closed," she whispered. She opened his shirt and ran her fingernails lightly across his broad, hairy chest. She kissed his neck then got off him, going back over to the suitcase. She grabbed her bag and headed down the stairs. "Everything you need is on the dresser, Bode. Give me fifteen minutes."

He sat up as he heard the bathroom door close. He walked over to the costume on the dresser. He finished taking off his shirt and jeans before stepping into the hairy suit; looking at himself in the mirror, he nearly laughed. The wolf suit had a washboard stomach and was wearing blue corduroy pants. *I look ridiculous,* he thought. I hope she makes this quick. He heard a door open, some shuffling in the kitchen, and then the back door opened and closed. He grabbed the giant wolf-head half-mask and walked downstairs.

Bode waited a few minutes before walking onto the back porch. He scanned the woods and saw Amelia's red cape about ten yards off. He walked toward the path then put on the mask, adjusting it so he could see where he was going.

He caught up with her a few minutes later. "Good morning."

Amelia turned around and smiled, a look of amusement quickly passing through her eyes. "Hello."

Bode's jaw dropped and he had trouble finding words.... All he could think about was Amelia and how sexy she looked in her costume. The garter dress had a white top with a red corset waist and a black, two-layered miniskirt. Thin puffed sleeves hung off her shoulders, and the hooded cape framed her heart-shaped face.

"A beautiful lady all alone in the woods...aren't you frightened?"

"No, Wolf, my cabin is only a short distance away, by the beautiful lake and willows. Do you know it?"

Bode smiled. "I do, but more flowers can always brighten a place up."

"You're right." Amelia picked up her basket and walked a few steps, her back turned to Bode. She bent over and picked up a green clover before coyly looking over her shoulder.

He stared. Amelia's asscheeks peeked from under the skirt when she bent over and the back seam of her white thigh-high stockings and black boots made her already long legs go on for miles. Bode didn't know if he'd make it back to the cabin when she bent over again. He turned and quickly followed the path back.

He rushed inside, leaving the door open, and went upstairs. Taking off the wolf suit, Bode left the mask on and jumped onto the bed. He got under the quilt and pulled it up to his shoulders as he heard Amelia in the kitchen.

"Hello?"

"I'm upstairs," he called.

Amelia slowly walked up the winding staircase, her heels clicking against the black iron. She reached the top, set her basket down and walked to the foot of the bed. "My, what large eyes you have."

"The better to see your beautiful body with."

She smiled. "My, what large hands you have."

"The better to touch you with."

Amelia crawled onto the bed, sitting on her knees. "My, what a large mouth you have."

"The better to please you with."

Bode ripped off the mask and sat up, gently laying Amelia down. He leaned over her, the quilt falling away from his body.

"My, what a large dick you have."

He smirked. "The better to fuck you with." He kissed her, his large hand trailing down her throat, between her breasts, down her sides and stopping on her thighs. He pulled away from her soft lips. "Strip for me, Red," he said gruffly.

Amelia smiled and stood up on the bed. She was so turned on by how excited Bode was when he saw her in the costume, and the look in his eyes, cloudy with anticipation. It gave her renewed sexual confidence. She gently put her left boot on Bode's chest, the chunky heel pressing into him. He untied it and slipped it off her foot, tossing the boot aside, then did the same with her other boot. She put her foot back down on his chest, as he rubbed her calf, feeling the muscle flex as she moved to keep her balance.

Amelia rolled her white stockings slowly over her knees, one at a time, running her fingers down the entire length of her legs while she did it. Bode started to sit up after she took off the second stocking, but she pushed him back down with her soft foot. She unlatched the silver clasp on the cape and ran it over his chest and dick. The touch of the cool velvet against his hot skin sent shivers down his spine.

She let it drop to the floor then walked off the bed. Bode sat on the edge and Amelia straddled his lap. She looked into his smoky blue eyes before leaning in to kiss his collarbone. Feeling his swelling thickness, Amelia delicately gyrated her hips on Bode's lap as she licked up the side of his neck. She nibbled his earlobe then raised her arms behind her to untie the top part of her costume, letting the long black ribbons fall down in between them. The corset top slid down a little showing more of her sexy cleavage. Bode grabbed her petite waist and kissed the top of her breasts before she was able to pull away.

She held his hands at his sides. "Not yet," she whispered and stood.

He needed to touch her, be inside of her. He didn't know how much more of the teasing he could take.

Amelia pulled her auburn locks forward and reached back to unzip the dress, slowly letting it fall to the floor.

When Bode saw the see-through red lace bra and ruffled panties, he rushed to her, grabbing her ass. She let out a giggle as he kissed her throat.

"You're incredibly sexy, Red."

She squeezed his ass and kissed his chest. Amelia pushed him onto the bed and straddled Bode again. She kissed his nipples and trailed down his chest, her hair lightly brushing his skin. She licked down his treasure trail then took his whole dick in her hot mouth. Bode sucked in a breath as she moved up and down his shaft, rolling her tongue around the tip. He pulled out before he exploded in her mouth. He wanted to hold out as long as he could.

He slid to the side and pulled Amelia next to him. He leaned over her, kissing her neck and collarbone as her nails gently scraped his shoulder blades. Bode moved down the center of her chest, blowing hot breath in between her tits. He quickly unfastened the front clasp of her bra, her beautiful breasts spilling out. He sucked her small pink nipples hard before moving his hand between her thighs, lightly rubbing across the lace of her panties. She let out a quiet moan of pleasure. Bode kissed her tight belly, delicately nibbling her soft skin as he went farther down her body.

He bit the waistband of her panties and pulled them down slightly before he licked her pelvic bone. Amelia lifted herself and helped him pull them all the way off. Bode planted light kisses on soft, trimmed pubic hair then plunged his tongue deep in her moist hole. She moaned again and lifted herself to meet his mouth. He slipped a long finger inside of her. Amelia started rubbing her clit, exciting him more. He needed to be inside of her, now.

"Oh, Bode."

He smiled as he saw her breath hitch.

She squeezed his bicep as she came in his mouth, wave after wave of delicious pleasure flowing over her. He licked all of her juices before lying down beside her.

Amelia caught her breath then took a condom off the nightstand. She rolled it over his erection and straddled his lap, gently lowering herself onto him. Bode grabbed her hips as she slowly gyrated on top of him. She reached down and rubbed her clit again as her tits lightly bounced with her movements. She started breathing heavily again as she rocked back and forth. He pulled her down on him hard, wanting to get as deep in her as he could. Bode felt her muscles clenching his shaft as she screamed his name. She fell onto him, her tits smashed against his chest, her skin on fire. He grabbed her tender ass and moved them both so that he was on top of her. She locked her ankles around his hips as he plunged deeper inside her. Bode bent over her, sucking her nipples as he slowed his thrusts, trying to delay his building orgasm. He ran his hand over her hips and his thumb found her clit, already hardening again.

Amelia pulled him closer to her with her legs. "Make me come again, Bode," she whispered.

His cock jumped at the challenge and he thrust harder and faster as he slowly traced circles on her clit. His balls tightened; Bode knew he couldn't hold out any longer.

Amelia held on to his back, her nails digging into him. She screamed his name again as another orgasm sent shivers throughout her body, exploding against Bode's thrusts. When he felt her muscles tighten around him, he finally released and came with her.

Bode deeply kissed her before lying down beside her. She rested her head on his shoulder and draped a slender arm across his heaving chest. He kissed the top of her head and ran his fingers through her long locks. "I love you, Amelia."

"I know," she murmured and smiled as she drifted into a peaceful sleep.

THE HOTEL

Anika Ray

So this is the plan, concocted last night through a haze of mutual daring and strong beer. Adam and I will meet at the F Bar and pretend to be strangers. After a night of flirting we will go home together. Everyone in the bar will think he is so suave. We will both be excited, since in fact we did not meet at a bar but at a church retreat, and neither of us has ever done anything like this before.

In theory—which often falls short—I am crazy with lust at the mere sight of him. In reality, being crazy with lust entails a little preparation, which I dutifully do. At lunchtime, I slip into the office bathroom and put on a pearl thong. This is a new invention—I imagine—that theoretically will stimulate my clit while I sit at my desk.

In reality, it pinches out several hairs, and I'm almost tempted to remove it until I lean over to pick up a paper that has fallen on the floor. Oh, wow. I drop a few more sheets, just for good measure. Again, yikes. I wiggle a little in my chair. My coworker

David gives me a strange look, or so it seems. I cross my legs, and the pearls really dig in.

We have agreed not to speak at all today. The thong digs into my soft clit, slips back and forth and feels alternately wonderful and painful; sometimes both at once. I am both wet and bruised.

At the end of the day I slip out the back door and hurry down to the gym locker room. I exchange my outfit for a black dress and high heels. I tap at my heavy clit and the blood rushes downward from my head. I'm feeling a little dizzy when I enter the hotel bar where we arranged to meet.

Perhaps because we're strangers tonight, the sight of his back facing me suddenly turns me on as if we had just started dating. Here is a man who is available for me, to claim with my body, although he doesn't know it yet. I walk into the bar and wait for him to sidle up beside me. I cross my legs and the thong sets my clit on fire once again. I can feel juice swishing between my lower lips.

"Excuse me," a deep voice says in my ear. I stiffen at once. But it's not him. "Let me buy you a drink," says the stranger, and when I turn to look for my handsome boyfriend he's still talking to someone else. A girl, as it so happens, which was not part of the plan. I suck an olive off the skewer in my martini glass and look into the stranger's gleaming orbs.

"Yes," I say, and accept another martini. Just shifting on my stool to face the newcomer kindles sweet agony. I'm afraid I'll have an orgasm right there on the chair and collapse into the unknown man's arms. My boyfriend had better hurry.

"So what do you do?" asks the man. He has a soft voice and clean nails, but feminine hands. Long thin fingers that look like pale fish. I think, traitorously, of one of those skinny clammy fingers flopping around inside me. The image is both delicious and off-putting.

"I...I'm a dancer," I say, because I know that this impresses men. He nods and takes a sip of his beer.

"I'm in the arts too," he nods. "A journalist."

Ooh.

"Arianna," I say, with a smile. Out of the corner of my eye I see Adam at last turn away from the swingy-haired brunette he was talking to. Our eyes meet and his widen before I cut my glance back to my companion.

"Jared," he says.

"Jared," I parrot, with another big sip of martini. Gosh, these drinks are strong. But it's not just the gin vision: Jared is attractive, in a feminine, slightly mysterious way. Unlike beautiful Adam, who has a cleft chin and a wide back, thick eyebrows and a deep chest.

Jared's body is probably smooth and pale. The thought arouses nothing more than my curiosity. The bud of my clit flares in thick blooms of blood, and for a moment I picture myself with Jared. What would we look like together? Would he push my legs apart with his narrow hands, like Adam does so easily with his stronger ones? Would he pin me beneath the heavy weight of his body, cross my legs around his muscular back? Lean over me, own me with his eyes?

I imagine he'd be a little more shy.

But why am I thinking about sex with another man right now? I try to focus. I'm annoyed at myself. Again, I catch Adam's eye over Jared's shoulder. His gaze is furious. It's a gaze I barely recognize. I didn't think he would mind, I tell myself. But I've never tried to make him jealous by flirting before.

Jared smiles at me, a smile full of male optimism. "So, are you from around here?" He toys with the lip of his beer bottle while I think.

"Nearby. But I'm staying in the hotel," I say, and eat another olive. My stomach feels warm, as does my lower body. I'm so hot I want to take off my dress. "You?"

"Far away. I'm just in town for the weekend." Our eyes meet, almost against my will, and without meaning to I realize we've just shared an understanding. Jared smiles, a warm sexy smile that brings out the light in his long, oval face.

"Excuse me," says a tight voice over Jared's shoulder. I turn into Adam's glacial stare. His lips are tight. His jaw seems to pulse. I have never seen him look this angry, and for a moment I'm afraid of what he'll do. "There's a call for you at the front desk."

"Oh." I cast Jared an apologetic look and before I can go, he reaches into his pocket and takes out a small rectangle. He flips it over, takes a pen from his pocket and writes something on the back.

"Call me if you're free while you're here," he says, and gives me that light lazy smile again. I feel angry heat rising off Adam's skin, and I've barely followed him out of the bar when he grabs my wrist in a grip so tight I'm worried I'll have bruises. He pulls us both into the employee bathroom and locks the door. I glance at the gold wallpaper and marble sink. It's a single stall. *Is he going to kill me?*

"Adam—" Before I can finish he lifts me and puts me down over the sink. Without meeting my eyes he flips up my black skirt. I don't know what's going through his mind. I look down on his suddenly unfamiliar head—covered in thick dark hair that I want to grab in my fists—as he stares at the sight in front of him. My nearly bare crotch, shiny lower lips bisected by two perfect strands of white pearls. He pushes the strands of pearls apart and rakes a rough finger between my lips. I shudder with pleasure and then realize what he must be thinking.

"I've been thinking about you all day," I whisper, so he

knows this is for him, it has nothing to do with Jared. But he doesn't even glance up.

"Good," he grunts. With his warm, dry palms he pushes my legs so far apart I'm afraid my hips will be sore tomorrow. He cups my ass in his hands, lifts it toward him and pushes his hard, thick cock into me.

"Oh, oh, oh," I gasp as his cock wiggles deeper and deeper, as if it has a mind of its own. From this angle it feels huge and thick, and my inner organs shift.

He wedges his cock all the way inside me and finally looks into my eyes. There's rage and lust boiling in that familiar gaze. An electric current rushes through me and my pussy clutches at his wide cock.

"Good," he says, and punctuates the word with a hard thrust that pushes me back against the sink. It feels so good I can't think or answer. I lean back as he moves in and out of me, punctuating his thrusts with groans or the occasional "Yes." Does he want to fuck the memory of tonight out of me?

We keep going, keeping up the awkward urgent rhythm. We've never done anything like this before, and I can't tell if he loves it as much as I do. In, out, back, forward; I'll have bruises from the faucet tomorrow but I don't care.

"Yeah," I urge him on, and he moves and I move forward against him and with a final shove I'm up against him and he lodges his cock all the way within me. My entire vagina becomes liquid. My expectant clit flares and throbs and I grab the faucet behind me for support as my legs and knees grow weak. "Oh, oh," I whisper, pulsing against him. A few moments later his hot come bubbles into me.

The sweat on my body cools. The haze before me clears and I realize where we are: in a bathroom at a hotel. I haven't even taken off my dress; he's still wearing his shirt. The front tails flap around his shrinking penis.

"Oh, my god," I mutter, climbing shakily off the sink. He grabs my elbow and starts laughing when I almost fall. The sound bubbles in the air, reminds me that he and I are still here, still the people we knew.

"Adam, are you—?" I ask suddenly, looking up at him, fear lancing through my veins. He's grinning like he just won the lottery.

"No, no," he dismisses my worry and pulls me against him for a long kiss. He tastes like alcohol. I love it. I lick the flavor off him.

"You're not mad?" I ask, when he lets me go. "No?"

"Naw," he says, shaking his head, and his funny grin doesn't budge.

"Was it an act?" I want to know.

"Yeah, yeah," he nods. But this time I catch a flicker of doubt in his eyes. Was he jealous or not? The thought that he might have been is a tiny delicious tingle in my stomach. It mixes with the afterglow of my orgasm and together we go out into the lobby again.

UNDERWEAR

Kay Jaybee

S traightening the black thigh-length skirt and matching jacket over her pristine white blouse, Leah checked her reflection one last time.

Finally satisfied with her look, Leah gathered her long chestnut hair into a neat ponytail, slipped her pumps onto her stocking-clad feet, grabbed the holdall that held a stack of catalogs advertising the cosmetics and underwear she sold and the items of lingerie her clients had ordered the week before, and headed out to work.

Smiling privately to herself, Leah knew the new underwear she wore beneath her suit was flattering her curvaceous figure, and she felt sexy and confident as she drove toward her target area, her mind lingering on one client more than the others.

Two hours, three sales and several positive enquiries later, Leah felt her pulse rate rise as she knocked on the door of his small terraced house. The door was opened almost the second she rang the bell.

"Good morning Mr. Richards, I have the underwear you ordered."

"You'd better come in." Leah walked into the narrow hallway and on into the living room, where she had spent a pleasantly flirtatious half an hour the week before.

He followed her, his alert blue eyes appraising her round figure; his tall frame towering over her as she sat on the edge of the sofa, the holdall on her knee already unclipped as she searched through its contents for his order.

"Here you go, Mr. Richards." Leah placed the see-through plastic bag on the coffee table. "One set of 36C/14 bra and knickers, crimson lace, with matching suspender belt and black stockings as per your request."

"Sam." His eyes twinkled as he spoke.

"Sam?"

"My name is Sam." He perched next to her. "Mr. Richards sounds a bit formal, don't you think?"

Inclining her head a fraction, but keeping her eyes lowered over her products, she replied, "I'm Leah." She could feel his eyes boring into her, and the tension in the room was pleasantly palpable as she fished her account book from her bag. "How would you like to pay?"

"Cash." He produced a battered wallet from his back pocket. "But first I'd like to make sure they fit."

All week Leah had indulged in the ridiculously unrealistic fantasy that this man was single, and that the underwear was for his sister or a friend. Feeling let down by her own flights of fancy, she said as lightly as she could, "Oh, is your girlfriend here, then?"

"No, she isn't, but you're about her size."

Leah laughed. "That's a bit cliché isn't it?"

"Maybe, but I'd still like to see you in it." He sounded serious, and as Leah risked a look at him, she could see he meant it.

"You have a girlfriend." Leah spoke with a finality she knew she didn't feel.

"Yes, I do." He reached a hand out and picked up the lingerie set. "But I still want to see you in this first."

"If I was your girlfriend, I wouldn't want you to give me preworn underwear."

"Lucky you're not my girlfriend then, isn't it?"

Leah's hand hesitated over her bag. She had no doubt he was serious, and she had even fewer doubts that her body was already reacting to the closeness of his presence, but that didn't make the fact of his girlfriend's existence disappear.

As if reading her mind, he said, "If I'd lied and said I hadn't got a girlfriend, would you be trying the undies on by now?"

Raising her gaze to meet his, Leah spoke with a defiant edge: "That's not the point. The fact is, you do have one; why else would you buy this stuff. It isn't exactly the sort of thing you'd buy your mother is it?"

"True." Sam stood back up. "It is also true that, spoken for or not, I haven't stopped thinking about you since last time you were here, and I've told my partner all about you."

Leah's stomach began to turn cartwheels as she forced herself to hold his stare, trying to ignore the feeling that she'd stumbled out of her depth. "You told her what exactly?"

He took another step nearer. "That I'd met a beautiful door-to-door lingerie seller, who I'd like to fuck."

Leah's calm exterior broke instantly at his confession. "You told your girlfriend that?"

"It surprises you that she'd rather I told her about encountering women I fancy, rather than keeping it quiet?"

The corners of Leah's mouth begin to curve as she struggled not to smile in incredulous disbelief. "Your honesty is indeed surprising." Closing her bag, Leah stood up. "I should go."

Trying not to inhale the delicious aroma of aftershave and sheer maleness that emanated from his creased shirt, Leah was forced to physically shove past Sam to reach the hallway, making her more aware of his height and bulk than ever before. She'd just reached the door when he said, "I haven't paid you yet."

Leah knew that if she was going to hold on to her principles, she had to leave now. "There's an address on the bill, you can mail me a check."

"Sarah will be so disappointed."

Something about his tone made Leah turn to face him. "Disappointed, why? You have her gift."

"No, I don't."

Her hand seemed to have frozen to the doorknob. Leah could feel her nipples hardening beneath her underwear; underwear that she knew was an exact match for the packet of lingerie Sam still held in his hand.

With a dry mouth, Leah stood there, statuelike. In two strides Sam was right next to her, close enough for her to feel his breath on her flesh.

Pushing her free hand into her jacket pocket and gripping the handle of her bag tightly with the other so that she couldn't reach out and pull his shirt from his jeans as she longed to, Leah said, "Explain."

"She wanted me to have you and then tell her all about it."

"What?"

Sam put a hand on her shoulder, and immediately Leah felt a treacherous rush of heat flow through her.

"She gets off on it, and naturally, so do I."

Attempting to deflect her concentration away from the pressure of his palm, Leah spoke with far more defiance than she felt. "And how do I know that you're not just saying that so you can get your leg over?"

"You don't." He stroked a finger across her cheek, sending tiny shock waves through her nervous system, "But I know you want to find out."

"You're an arrogant git aren't you?"

Sam smiled. "Yeah, I am, and I still want to see you in that underwear."

Leah leveled her eyes firmly into his. If she was going to do this, she was going to do it on her terms, not his, "If I do this, I'm not coming back here again. Not ever."

His eyes blazed with a swift flash of victory, but wisely he said nothing, merely nodding his head.

Throwing her shoulders back, Leah walked back to the living room, ignoring the voice at the back of her head telling her to get the hell out of there and listening only to her body, which wanted her client's cock inside her as soon as possible, girlfriend or no girlfriend.

Determined to rob Sam of his assumed control, Leah thumped her bag onto the coffee table, and with her heart beating fast, and her hands on her hips, said, "Right, stay exactly where you are. Do not move."

Sam looked more amused than put out and obediently stayed in the doorway between the hall and the living room.

"If you want to see me in that underwear, then you can."

Dropping her jacket to the ground, Leah maintained eye contact with Sam. If she looked away she was afraid that her courage would fail her, or worse, she'd start to think about what she was actually doing. Placing a hand on either side of her skirt, she eased it to the floor, giving her solo audience the first indication that she was already attired as per his wishes.

Sam's arms dropped to his sides as he watched her, and he

leaned more heavily against the door frame. Encouraged by the hunger in his eyes, Leah moved her attention to the small pearl buttons of her shirt. As she undid the top fastening, Sam gave an audible gasp, which made Leah speed up, and soon her top joined the clothes on the floor.

The voice at the back of her head was shouting now, telling her how important it was to keep control, to make him wait. Tilting up her chin, Leah said, "So, what do you think of the underwear?"

"Gorgeous." Sam lurched forward, so that they stood either side of the coffee table. "I knew it would look better on you than in a lifeless packet."

Leah moved her hands so that her fingers could trace the lacy outline of her bra. "It certainly feels good to wear."

Sam almost whispered, "Are you the same size as Sarah then? I hoped you were."

"It would appear I am." Leah took one hand from her chest and placed a single digit inside the top of her panties and ran it over the belly beneath. "The question is, what do you look like in your underwear?"

Sam's jeans were off so quickly that Leah had to struggle not to giggle at his eagerness and shatter the whole "in control" illusion she'd been building up. Observing him closely as crisp black boxers appeared from beneath his trousers, and his shirt hit the table, she felt her crotch twitch with erotic anticipation.

His underwear was smart, designer with three little buttons at the fly, and more importantly, a telling bulge beneath. "Nice."

"Thanks."

Neither of them moved, the table acting as a barrier between them.

Leah licked her lips as the tension in the room continued to rise. "Your girlfriend must be a very unusual woman."

"Sarah is one of a kind. I'm very lucky."

"And you really are going to tell her how you fucked me?"

"Exactly how..." Sam knocked the holdall and new underwear from the table, sending them flying toward the hall, and knelt on the unyielding wood, reaching his hands out to Leah's chest. "Action for action, groan for groan, climax for climax."

With a massive effort of will, Leah took hold of his wrists and lifted his palms from her breasts, stifling the whine of loss she felt when the removal of his exploring fingers left her feeling dangerously neglected.

"And how will she feel when you report that rather than you take me..." Picking up his shirt, Leah twisted it into a long sausage shape and moved to the other side of the table. "...I took you?"

Deftly positioning her client's unresisting arms behind his back and tying his shirt around his wrists, Leah instructed him to stand.

Sam, a sly grin on his face, said nothing, but simply waited, curious to see what the saleswoman planned to do next.

"Sit on the edge of the table." Leah stood between his outstretched legs, glancing at the cock that was evidently stiffening further beneath his shorts.

She'd fantasized about having sex with this man all week, and although Leah hadn't really believed her dream would come true, she had a good idea of what she wanted to do.

Placing her hands on his shoulders, she trailed her painted fingernails down each side of his smooth chest, lingering over his stiff nipples, flicking their tips once or twice, watching with fascination as they hardened into short peaks.

All the time Leah sensed Sam looking at her, his eyes boring into the top of her head. It wouldn't have taken much effort for him to break free from his restraints, but he made no attempt to escape as Leah slid her hands farther south, exploring the outline of his toned torso down to his naval, which she circled with light scratches of his skin.

Dropping to her knees, she bought her mouth to his stomach. With long lingering laps that made him tighten his muscles further, she tongued his flesh an inch above the elastic of his underwear. Encouraged by the growl Sam wasn't able to contain, Leah's kisses became firmer as she gripped his knees to steady herself, her chest rubbing against the lace that encased it.

Drawing back, Leah brought her eyes back to his. The ache in her chest was becoming unbearable; she felt as if her breasts were actually inflating. Placing her hands behind her back, she unfastened her bra and finally freed her tits from captivity. Sam's eyes widened at the sight of her creamy freckled chest and large nipples, which were pointing directly at him, as though they were accusing him of something.

Leah began to weigh her tits in her palms, easing a single finger up and over each, making herself gasp as she caressed her body in front of her semibound audience.

Following every move of Leah's masturbation, Sam gulped as one hand entered her knickers. He stared as she closed her eyes, the hand obviously manipulating her mound, hidden by the red lace. Sam's cock pressed painfully into his thigh. He wasn't going to be able to take much more before he would have to have his own underwear removed; plus, although Leah was blissfully unaware of the fact, time was running out.

His breath caught in his throat as, with her eyes still closed, Leah hooked either side of her knickers beneath her thumbs and edged them to the floor. Ideally he would have liked to see this through, to see what this amazing woman planned for his domination, but he had instructions of his own to carry out.

It took only a matter of seconds to release his hands, and while Leah was lost in her personal world of pleasure, Sam picked up his shirt and Leah's blouse, tearing his eyes away from Leah, and stood up.

Sensing movement, Leah's eyes flashed open, but Sam was too quick for her. In seconds she'd been picked up and pushed, back down, against the large coffee table, a knee pinning her stomach in place, while her right hand was yanked up and attached to a table leg with his shirt.

Shocked by the dramatic turn of events, Leah's left wrist was already being restrained before her voice came to her. "What the fuck are you doing?"

"Taking control." He stunted any further protests with his mouth, kissing her ferociously. "Trust me. This, you will love."

Leah's head spun; she'd been moments from orgasm, and she longed to come. She pulled at her arms, but the bindings held, and as he spread her legs wide and attached her ankles to the table legs, she realized that he'd had as many plans for her as she'd had for him.

Robbed of the ability to move, Leah felt incredibly vulnerable. No one had ever secured her so completely; a natural control freak, she was always the one who did the tying up. This was new territory, and she wasn't sure if she was thrilled or terrified.

Sam swung a leg over the table and stood astride the tethered woman, his dick still a prisoner in his underwear. "You look amazing." He leaned forward and freed Leah's hair from its ponytail, so that she could rest her neck more comfortably against the wood.

Leah was about to speak, when he placed his warm lips over her right tit, and her words of protest immediately morphed into a drawn-out mewl, and her sensation was increased when a hand came to her other breast, teasing the slightly rough skin around the areola.

A gentle click bought Leah back to reality, and she pointlessly struggled to sit up. "What was that?"

"Nothing," Sam murmured through his mouthful of breast, and Leah sank back against the table. Her hair was already a mass of knots beneath her as her head moved from side to side in frustration at not being able to touch him and confusion at her body's total enjoyment of being entirely at the whim of someone else.

As Sam worked, Leah could feel the climax she'd been denied rise again, increasing in urgency with every lap of his tongue and each flick of his fingers. "Don't stop, please don't…I'm so close."

Sam kept going, his ears listening for the quickening of her breath that would tell him Leah could take no more. He was also listening for another sound, the sound of a packet being opened.

Leah's back began to arch against the table. "Oh, hell, Sam, I'm coming, I'm gonna…"

"Not yet you're not."

Sitting up abruptly Sam looked toward the hall, the shift in his weight forcing Leah against the unyielding surface of the coffee table. "You took your time."

Leah felt cold, as if someone had pressed the PAUSE button on her orgasm, while her brain struggled to make sense of what her eyes told her was happening.

"You look fantastic sweetheart." Sam beamed at Sarah, who stood in the doorway dressed in her brand-new lingerie.

Blinking, trying to extinguish the vision in front of her, Leah forced herself to digest the knowledge that she should have seen this coming. Horribly self-conscious of her nakedness, she wriggled against her restraints.

"Don't bother, honey." Sarah swept her stunning red hair from her shoulders as she peered down at the saleswoman. "If Sam has tied you up, he'll have done it securely enough to make sure you can't escape."

Her throat had never felt drier, and yet Leah could feel the liquid continue to leak from her pussy as two sets of eyes focused all their attention on her prone body.

Sarah put out a hand and yanked Sam off Leah's stomach, so that they were next to each other. As if she was a lioness marking her mate, Sarah kissed him deeply, leaving Leah in no doubt as to whom this man belonged. Then, glancing at Leah again, Sarah said, "You're right Sam, she is beautiful."

Leah's face turned from pink to scarlet as the other woman casually placed a hand, flat and unmoving, between her legs. "Tell me, Sam, what's happened so far? What have I missed?"

Feeling like a thing, a mere object, a sex toy for two lovers, Leah listened as Sam gave Sarah a blow-by-blow account of everything they'd done together. As he told his lover about Leah's masturbation, she laughed, and Leah felt the blush on her face creep through her and swamp the rest of her shamed flesh.

Attempting to block out the conversation going on above her, Leah shut her eyes, but there was no escape from either the audible replay, or the pressure of the gloriously soft palm that remained fixed in place between her legs.

When Sam eventually stopped talking, Leah cautiously dared to open her eyes. The silence between the three of them was tense, the expressions of her companions unreadable. Leah felt the need to speak, to break the heavy expectant atmosphere that floated around the room. "You look nice."

Even as she spoke, Leah knew her comment had been rather lame, but Sarah smiled. "Thank you, so do you..." She started to glide her hand gently up and down. "...And you feel even better."

Leah moaned softly as her body leapt a little off the table. Immediately, Sarah removed her hand, making Leah whimper in distress.

Losing another chance to orgasm deprived Leah of the last vestiges of her pride, as Sarah adopted the position Sam had previously held over her hips, placing her hands on her own chest. "It's gorgeous, this underwear you sell, but don't you find that the lace edging is a little scratchy?" Without bothering to let Leah reply, Sarah pulled the bra's cups beneath her tits and began to fondle her nipples. "How badly do you want to suck these I wonder? As badly as you want your own chest sucked I should think, but perhaps not as badly as you want Sam's dick in your pussy?"

Leah gazed up at the other woman, her brain racing. She'd been with women before, but not like this, not without some level of power, and not for a very long time.

"No answer?" Sarah continued to play with her breasts. "Perhaps you aren't that bothered about coming after all?"

"What? No! I have to, please..."

Sarah laughed again, but more kindly this time, as she turned to Sam. "Time to remove those boxers, honey, before they cripple you for life."

Swiftly Sam obliged, and Leah sighed at the sight of him: his cock was as hard as any she'd ever seen.

Sarah pointed, and Sam went to the foot of the table, crouching by Leah's tethered feet. Then, moving so she stood over Leah's head, leaning forward so that her breasts hovered just inches from Leah's lips, Sarah spoke bluntly: "Suck me."

As she engulfed the offered right nipple, a zip of electricity instantly shot through Leah at the sensation of having a woman's breast in her mouth. Then, as she got into a comfortable rhythm of licks and nips, Leah jolted again; a male tongue was working between her legs.

It only took a few seconds before the orgasm Leah had been denied twice before raced up her throat and along her spine. As her pussy quivered against Sam's greedy mouth, Leah's cries of pleasure were muffled by Sarah pushing her tit farther into her mouth.

Exhausted, Leah felt the final flutters of her climax escape, and her kisses against Sarah's peach skin became lighter as the strain in her neck and the ache in her trapped body filled her with sudden fatigue.

Stroking a hand across Leah's forehead, Sarah wiped away stray strands of hair before she signaled to Sam to untie their guest. Then they helped Leah to sit up and allowed her to catch her breath for a moment, before Sam abruptly picked her off the table and laid her on the sofa.

Seconds later, Sarah was astride Leah's face, and Sam was over her hips, his cock pumping in and out of her as Sarah ordered, "Lick me girl; make me come."

Flashing colors danced behind Leah's eyes as she worked her tongue frantically over Sarah's clit, while the gloriously thick dick of the client she'd fantasized about all week rammed in and out of her. A new climax knocked the first from Leah's mind with sharp intensity, as Sam came in her and Sarah spasmed wonderfully sticky juice across her lips and chin.

They left the underwear seller to dress on her own. As Leah picked up her discarded holdall she noticed that a pile of cash had been left next to her bag; precisely the correct amount for Sarah's new underwear.

Feeling wobbly on her kitten heels, she took a final look

around the room, her eyes lingering for a moment on the coffee table, picturing what she must have looked like to her client and his girlfriend. Smiling to herself, Leah headed quietly to the front door.

Her hand was on the latch when Sam came up behind her. "Sarah really loves that underwear."

"Good." Leah didn't know what else to say.

"She wondered if you had another set of the same style in black."

"I'll have to order it, but yes."

"Will you bring it next week?"

"I said I'd never come back."

"I know what you said, but will you bring it next week anyway?"

Leah fixed her eyes directly on Sam's. "Maybe," she said, before she walked out the door and headed to her car, knowing as well as he did that she'd be back.

ALL
SHAVED UP

Liv Olson

M illie plugged in the hair trimmer and stepped into the tub. She flipped the switch and the low burring noise started. She looked down and began to quickly run the trimmer over her pussy—zip, zip, zip; one, two, three—right from the top down to the point of her dark Bermuda triangle.

Amazing how easily she shaved the most intimate part of her body now, she thought, compared to the first few times she'd attempted it. And that first time took the cake. She struggled to recall why she decided to try shaving. She'd resisted the idea for a long time. One boyfriend asserted she was "medium hairy" and suggested she shave "only if she wanted to…." Another had barged into her apartment practically demanding that she do so. Why did men get turned on by seeing women shaved up? It seemed so trashy to her—all related to fulfilling some kinky male sex fantasy.

Then she met Brad. His body hair spoke of southern European stock. Not swarthy or especially hirsute, he had plenty of dark curly hair on his chest and arms and legs and—well—down there. Or at least he appeared as if he would, should he so desire. The first time Millie and Brad lay bare chest to bare chest, she realized he must be trimming his chest hair—with scissors. He claimed short hair kept him cooler, more comfortable. She fought against scratching. Pokey, pointy, jaggedly cut chest hairs created an uncomfortable environment for snuggling. Brad cut his chest hair with scissors about as well as Millie trimmed her long-gone Lhasa Apso with scissors—the result was functional but definitely not aesthetic. If the poor dog had had any pride, it would have wilted in public.

Then Brad decided to experiment with a hair trimmer. The first time he used it, Millie thought she'd died and gone to heaven. His chest felt ever so much better. She never minded curly chest hair in the first place, but if he wanted it short, she definitely preferred uniformly trimmed hair.

Then the trimmer kept moving lower and lower.

And Millie decided she kind of liked it—Brad's being shaved up. They were nice, even haircuts. She could see the patterns in his hair, the whorls around the nipples, the strokes pointing toward his member—like a Van Gogh painting: dark brush-strokes on a pale canvas.

So she asked Brad to trim her up too.

Millie pulled her labia apart to get the finer hair at the inner edge, fingers protecting her delicate areas: zip, zip, zip. She grimaced at herself for waiting so long.

The first time Millie tried to shave down there, she nearly chickened out, scared to death of cutting herself in a most uncomfortable location. So she asked Brad to do it. They spread out a towel on his bed and she lay on it naked. The big orange extension cord was strung from the bathroom into the bedroom.

"Are you ready?" Brad asked her.

Millie's eyes widened and she nodded.

Brad turned the clipper on and she heard the buzz.

"I don't know if I'm ready for this," she said. "Is it going to hurt? What if you cut Martha?"

"Martha?"

"You know. Martha."

"You call it 'Martha'?"

"Well, you call yours 'Mr. Johnson'!"

Brad rolled his eyes. "I'm using a guide on the clipper," he said. "It makes sure the blades don't get too close to anything important."

"Okay," Millie said, tensing up. "Go ahead."

Brad brought the clipper to her belly.

"Here," he said, "I am just going to rest it on your tummy so you can feel it. It isn't going to hurt you—or Martha."

She felt the vibrations of the clipper on her lower belly, not yet touching her hair. She'd had the back of her neck trimmed up in the past, but it had been a long time since she'd had hair that short. And she had never worried about her neck the way she worried about Martha.

"Okay, I'm going to start with just a little at the top."

Brad pressed the flat edge of the trimmer against her firmly, right where the line of hair started. He went about an inch then stopped and looked at her.

"That feels weird," she said.

He did another swipe on either side of the first one. And another. After he'd trimmed the entire upper part of her pussy, he stopped.

"Are you ready for me to go lower?" he asked.

Millie nodded. Then shook her head, then nodded again.

"Okay," she said. "Do it."

Brad spread her legs farther apart. As he brought the clipper close to her, Millie yelped.

"What? I didn't even touch you yet."

"I know. I'm just nervous."

"Okay, hold still." Brad tried again.

Just as the clipper touched her skin, Millie yelped again.

Brad stepped back and looked at her sternly.

"I can't do this if you're going to keep squawking like that," he said.

Millie's eyes widened farther. "You can't leave me like this!"

"Then hold still!"

"I'll try," she said.

But of course she couldn't. Every time Brad touched her, she winced, or yelped, or squeezed her eyes shut and made a sound like an injured dog. It took almost half an hour for Brad to finish. No damage to Martha.

Millie lifted her leg a bit so she could reach the hair trimmer deeper down, past the labia toward her ass, trimming the hair along the crevice. She did it all by feel: first one side, then the other.

Millie remembered how she got aroused the first time Brad shaved her up, despite her fear of potential injury. She didn't realize how much the attention to that region of her body would affect her. Though the intent of the experiment was entirely nonsexual, the looking and touching and moving bits and pieces out of the clipper's way got her wet. Brad must have noticed along the way, but he didn't say anything.

"Go rinse off," he ordered as he wrapped up the extension cord.

While she showered, Millie felt the swelling of her cunt, the slipperiness exuding from her opening. The realization that shaving turned her on surprised her. When Millie returned from the shower, Brad lay on the bed naked, stroking himself.

"God, it turns me on to see you naked. To shave you up and see you get all hot and wet while I'm doing it," he said.

"Me, too. How did that happen?"

"You have a pretty little pussy," he said, "and I think you like showing it off!"

"No, I don't!" said Millie. "That's not why I did this!"

"Are you sure?" Brad asked. He smiled—or smirked—she couldn't quite tell which.

Maybe he was right, she thought. She climbed on top of him and settled herself on his cock. She couldn't stop thinking about having him look at her so closely. Her cunt dripped with sweet juice. She hovered over him, moving her bottom up and down, touching him only with her pussy. She liked the feeling of connectedness through open space. As she moved on his cock, he reached up and placed his hands on her breasts, cupping them, squeezing them with the rhythm of her movement.

As she got closer to climax, Millie shifted her weight so only Brad's tip remained inside her and she began to move faster, enjoying the sensations on the delicate flesh of her opening. Brad dropped his hands back to the bed. Millie knew he liked to close his eyes in order to concentrate on the fullness of her warmth and wetness and rhythm that led to his explosion. This time, however, he propped himself up so he had a good view of his crown being swallowed by her lips. She continued her quick movements on his tip, then plunged him into her all the way. She paused—and now his eyes squeezed shut as he came. Millie started to move harder, knocking herself against Brad as he spurted, hitting that sweet spot inside of her with a violence that caused her to yelp once more as she felt herself reach her peak. She gave a warranted yelp this time.

She collapsed on Brad, her body motionless except for her heaving chest. After a moment, she lifted her head. Brad smiled at her.

"Well," she said smiling back, "if that is what it is like to get shaved up, I might have to do it more often."

She had to admit, she liked shaving. Brad was right—a trim pussy kept her cooler, more comfortable. Once in a while she missed being able to brush her hair smooth, but, hey, whoever saw it brushed? And it never stayed that way. Now she just buzzed herself up every couple of weeks. She didn't even use a guard anymore. Just all the way down. But she wouldn't even think of attempting a razor. She could only go so far.

Millie looked at her shorn pussy again. She liked to see that apex where the lips meet, drawing the viewer to the inner sanctum. She knew Brad would stiffen at the sight of her exposed flower. Although now the process was old hat, she still enjoyed the view of her freshly shaved pussy each time. She liked how chic it looked: not bare skin like a little girl, but trim and tight like a well-put-together woman. She was a strong woman. She was in control of her life. Except when she wasn't—and that kind of out-of-control took place with Brad.

"Ahem," came a voice.

She looked up to see Brad standing there watching her with his staff at full mast.

"Wanna shave me up?" he asked, stepping into the tub.

"Seriously?" she asked.

He nodded.

"Okay," Millie replied.

She started with his chest, methodically moving the trimmer across his pecs. She kneeled in the tub to continue down to his belly. She noticed the little appendectomy scar that reappeared every time his hair was shorn. She continued down to his lower belly and pubic hair. His cock stared her in the face, rock-hard and red. She felt her own sex organs responding.

"How about I do the rest. Here," he said as he squirted some shave gel in her hands, "put this on the boys." She complied, swirling the gel into foam. He picked up his razor. Tightening his scrotum, he careful ran the razor over his balls.

She couldn't believe it. She didn't think she could ever get a sharp blade that close to her private parts. She watched in fascination as he moved the razor to the base of his cock where he cleaned up a few hairy stragglers. Millie had never seen this part of the process before. Her pussy pulsed already from shaving herself and now it responded to Brad's actions.

When Brad finished, he turned on the shower. They rinsed off without a word. He flipped the water back off. They stared at each other until Millie felt Brad pull her out of the tub and lay her on the rug in front of the sink, still wet.

He positioned himself over her and quickly pushed his cock into her wet pussy.

Oh, what a relief, she thought. Her internal pressure had built to such a level that she felt like her sex would turn inside out without Brad's cock to keep it in place. She moaned.

He began thrusting with urgency, slamming into her again and again, and she bucked back against him.

After what felt like only a moment—or a month—she exploded. The visual and tactile stimulation had raised her sensitivity to an all-time high. Brad followed her shortly thereafter, with a loud grunt as he erupted inside her. One, two, three, four, five strong strokes and then he suspended his motion; she could feel his cock continuing to pulse against the walls that held him so tight.

There they lay, wet from the shower, sweaty from their exertion, limp from their climax. Millie pictured Brad's shaft in her face as she shaved his belly, her hands foaming up his balls, his fingers delicately tightening his sac.

"Well," Millie said, "if that's what it's like to shave you up, I might have to do that more often."

NEW DAY, NEW LIFE

Andrea Dale

So, is it everything you hoped for?" Mike asked.

Rachelle snuggled beneath his arm. "And more," she said. "I'm here, with you, and I'm healthy. It doesn't get much better than that."

Here was Prague; specifically, the wide pedestrian Charles Bridge, the perfect place for a stroll after a dinner of smoked pork and dumplings and cabbage and velvety smooth beer.

The summer's night air was a soft caress on her skin. Accents and foreign words slipped around them like the slow-flowing Vltava River under the bridge. Ahead, the Old Town buildings were softly lit.

She was content. She was alive.

The bout with cancer had terrified her, but she'd met the terror head-on and come out the other side relatively unscathed. She'd been given a clean bill of health—a second chance. And, as she'd told her husband, she wanted to do all the things she'd thought about doing but set aside due to work or commitments or time.

Mike, being as astounding a husband as she could ever hope for, had agreed.

So they'd come to Eastern Europe, land of her forebears. She didn't care about the direct genealogy—too far back to follow—but since she'd been a girl she'd wanted to see the places with the exotic-sounding names and pastel-colored buildings and paprika-laced food.

She wanted to experience it.

They wandered to a stop at the end of the bridge, found an empty spot along the rail next to one of the many monuments that lined the wide stone walkway. Light from a nightclub that jutted out into the river made sparkles on the water. Maybe they'd play Poohsticks tomorrow, if they could find some twigs.

"Well, you don't see that every day," Mike said.

The nightclub had several curved windows—alcoves, if you were inside—and spotlighted in each was a dancer, facing out into the night.

A naked dancer, save for her tiny G-string and spike-heeled go-go boots.

"No," Rachelle said, "you certainly do not."

Normally she would have added, "Not in the nice part of town," but somehow, this just didn't seem as sleazy as she would have expected. The nightclub was obviously modern and upscale, and while it clashed with its surroundings, it (and the dancers) didn't strike her as sordid. Different cultures had different standards.

The closest dancer either had incredibly long hair or wore an extension, because the ends of her high ponytail brushed the middle of her bare back. She was lean without being skinny, with natural-looking breasts. Her boots and thong were electric blue. Her movements were fluid, graceful, as she danced to music the onlookers couldn't hear.

That was about all Rachelle could see from this distance.

"You seem quite mesmerized with her," Mike commented.

And Rachelle realized she'd been staring at the dancer for a good five minutes.

"Oh," she said. "Well. She's very good."

Mike leaned over her shoulder, his lips brushing against her neck. She shivered under the delicious feel of his kisses. His breath ruffled her hair as he said, "I think it's more than that, darling."

At home—*before*—she might have laughed his words away. But she'd learned not to shy away from anything anymore. Life was too short for denial, even denying something to oneself.

That didn't make it easy, of course. But it was dark, and they were alone in their little alcove, and most people walking by wouldn't have understood what they were saying anyway. And Mike loved her without reservation.

The Chinese characters for *fear* and *excitement,* she'd been told, were the same.

Deep breath. "I've always...found other women attractive," she said.

His arms tightened in a hug around her waist. "I've noticed. I've always appreciated that you didn't get jealous when I looked at a pretty woman—and that you sometimes said she was pretty, too. Go on."

She wanted to squirm, but faced things head-on. "It's more than just appreciating the female form, although that's definitely part of it. I did have one...I guess you'd call it an encounter, in college. We didn't go all the way. Whatever that means when it's two women." She laughed, releasing nervous energy.

"Anyway, we were drunk, which gave me the courage to play, and we kissed and fondled. But that was about it."

"Did you come?" Mike whispered. She could feel his cock hardening against her tailbone, and she shivered again, deep inside where it counted.

"Not during. I was pretty worked up, though, and I masturbated when I got back to my room. It's all a bit fuzzy, really. I never had the guts to follow through on anything afterward."

It wasn't just Mike's hands sliding up her rib cage to cup the underside of her breasts and then higher to graze over her nipples, harder and more sensitive than she'd realized they'd become; it was also his next words that made her inner walls clench.

"Do you want to now?" he asked.

She had to think about that. Thinking was hard enough when he was caressing her nipples; now he was rolling them gently between his fingers. The thin knit of her sweater and the satin of her bra muted the sensations, but that didn't make them any less delicious.

Any less maddening.

"Um," she said. "Well, on a purely physical level, maybe. Yes. But there's also the rational and logical and emotional levels. I prefer men; I need a man in my life to balance me. More importantly, I love you, and I married you, and I promised to be faithful to you. I'm not going to throw that away."

"I love you, too," he said. "Without reservation. But if monogamy weren't an issue—if, say, hypothetically we both agreed to the parameters and rules—then what would you say?"

Warmth and heat spread through her. He was rock-solid hard against her, and she wanted to turn and fold herself around him, but it all felt so good. She couldn't help but wriggle her hips back against him, and the graze of his teeth against her neck told her how that affected him.

"I'd say there were still some emotional issues to contemplate," she said. "It's...complicated."

"I can see that," Mike said, his fingers working her nipples more firmly, making her want to rip off her top and bra and toss them in the river so she could feel the cool night air and his hands against her heated skin.

"How about this," he went on. "For right now—this moment, here, us—we'll just think about it. How it might go, how it might be." His voice turned husky. "Confess to me, Rachelle."

So she did. The words spilled out of her, and she didn't censor them or try to form them into a coherent narrative. She talked about how it felt in college, soft small hands on her, narrow, delicate fingers; smooth skin, the only hair a peachy fuzz; warm lips, questioning and exploring rather than possessing.

Although there was possessing, too.

As she talked about pretty women and stared, sometimes unseeing, sometimes rapt, at the dancer in the window across the water, Mike's hands were on her.

He murmured in her ear, encouraging her on when she faltered, as he slowly gathered the fabric of her long, flowing skirt in his fingers, drawing it up to her waist. From behind, it still hung low and proper (as if anyone would try to peer past Mike's legs to gauge).

And it was dark. And they were in a foreign country where nobody knew them, and an exotic dancer blithely undulated for the world to see. And the air on her legs only reminded her how deliciously naughty what they were doing was.

Her tiny thong was useless, drenched. Mike slipped his fingers around it, finding no resistance. He dipped into the heat and wet of her, and she hissed, wanting more. Instead, he drew his hand away, up.

In the glow of a nearby streetlight she could see his fingers glistening. He painted them along her lips, whispering something about how incredible and sweet a woman tastes, and did she want to taste that? She moaned, and he took the opportunity of her parted mouth to edge inside, and she sucked the taste of herself, which *was* incredible and sweet.

As she watched the dancer writhe, she let herself freefall into sensation. Mike was stroking her again, not just teasing this time but focusing, his fingers sliding across her clit. Every muscle in her thighs and calves quivered as she balanced on the edge of need and with the need to keep standing.

And then, blessedly, she was coming, hard and contracting and so very alive.

She wasn't entirely clear on how they made it back to their hotel and had only a vague sense of stumbling through the lobby, riding up on the tiny clanking elevator, groping like teenagers.

She felt drunk on life and vacation and arousal. She couldn't imagine how Mike had made it all the way back; he was still so hard. He stripped off his shirt even as she parted his pants, drew out his cock and took it into her mouth.

It was blissfully hard, yet she couldn't help comparing the solid rigidity, the coarse hair and taut muscles of his thighs, with her hazy memory of touching the woman in college. Neither better, just...different.

Mike urged her up to kneel on the bed; flipped her skirt up and divested her of the useless thong. Just before he slipped the glorious length of him inside of her, as he teased her still-wet, still-needy sex with the head of his cock, he said, "Imagine that dancer lying in front of you, legs spread, desperate for you to touch her."

Then he was inside of her, stroking deep and firm. She was spiraling higher, lingering on the edge. The image he described shimmered into a vision and cradled between that and Mike, she let go and came.

The next morning, they ordered room service, a typical Czech breakfast of dark rye bread and salami and cheese and coffee. Lounging against the feather pillows, Rachelle asked Mike if he wanted her to explore her bi side so he could sleep with another woman. She didn't expect him to have an ulterior motive, far from it. She just wanted to know how he felt about the whole thing.

He had to think about it, and she nibbled bread and cheese and sipped her coffee, feeling...content, almost light.

"I think," Mike said finally, "yes, that's probably part of it. There's always a thrill to being with someone new and different. I'm not looking for that—it's not a part of my life anymore— but I have to acknowledge that aspect of it. The real reason, I'm pretty sure, is that you look so damn beautiful when you come, and I'd love to see that happen with another woman, so I can just enjoy how you look and react and cry out with passion."

Rachelle had to put down her coffee cup before she spilled the hot liquid everywhere.

That day, she noticed women everywhere; not more women, but more detail: the curves and lines; the smooth skin, kohl-rimmed eyes, manicured nails, hair thick or thin, straight or curled, short or long; the graceful gesture of a hand; the crinkles of laughter at the corner of the eyes and mouth; a full lower lip, the sway of hips.

She almost missed the sightseeing, lost in the wonder of what she was seeing, she almost felt like, for the first time. Or was it remembering, a part of her coming awake after a long slumber? Sleeping Beauty seeing the beauty.

She was distracted. How did men get through the day? There were so many breasts to ogle, asses to admire, legs to lust after. She was thankful for her sunglasses, hiding her lustful gaze.

All the looking at women and admiring women and, let's face it, imagining women naked and wanting, meant she couldn't escape the question that plagued her: Did she want to sleep with another woman?

She wanted to experience it again, yes. She had enough faith in the strength of her marriage to contemplate it, yes.

The fact that they were in a faraway foreign country meant it would be easier to do it with no attachments, no strings. Nobody would know or possibly even care.

If she and Mike agreed to the parameters...

She contemplated suggesting she have a tryst alone—have her experience, be done with it. But the more she contemplated that, the less it appealed to her. If she was going to do this, she wanted to share it with Mike.

The day after that, *maybe* solidified into *yes*.

They'd talked a little more the previous night, over wine with dinner and a nightcap in the quiet corner bar where Czech folk music enclosed them in a private bubble.

She thought, that night, when she went to sleep, she was sure.

She wasn't so sure the next morning.

Then they met Eliska.

It seemed a little too obvious, like something in a letter written in a trashy magazine. They'd gone to St. Vitus Cathedral, as part of a tour they'd arranged ahead of time. There were ten people on the tour, which was led by Eliska.

She was, hands down, the best tour guide they'd had in any monument in any country.

In accented but excellent English, she told them about the cathedral's—and, by extension the Czech Republic's—history, not by reciting facts and dates and lineages, but by telling stories. She engaged the listeners, encouraging them, for example, to look for motifs throughout the building (carved in stone, depicted in stained glass, embroidered in cushions and tapestries) even as she wove the meanings of the motifs into her monologue.

Rachelle *did* pay attention, because it was all quite fascinating. But at the same time, she found herself watching Eliska, too.

She had thick, pale brown hair that she piled atop her head in a Gibson-girl bun, tendrils curling madly everywhere. She wore pointy-toed, kitten-heeled shoes; the heels clicked as she walked with a brisk stride. Her laugher was soft but infectious, and she had one of the most open smiles Rachelle had ever seen.

Their group was small—besides the two of them, there was a family of four, an older couple and their teenagers, and not one of them really seemed all that interested. So Eliska responded more personally to Rachelle and Mike, because they were paying attention, asking questions, evincing curiosity.

At least, that's what Rachelle told herself.

"We should give her a good tip," Mike whispered at one point, and Rachelle agreed—for both the right and the wrong reasons, she freely admitted to herself.

It was the last tour of the day, and Rachelle assumed that would be the end of it. She'd have a satisfactory fantasy about Eliska with Mike when they were back at the hotel, and when they returned home, she'd open herself to finding a woman who might want to join them for a night.

But then Mike told Eliska that Rachelle's family was Czech, and Eliska turned bright eyes on Rachelle.

"Really? What was their name?"

Rachelle stumbled over the pronunciation, feeling awkward in her sudden crush.

"That's not an uncommon name, but it's one that does go far back in our history," Eliska said. "Some were involved with the building of this cathedral, even."

"We'd love to hear more," Mike said. "Can we bribe you to join us for drinks?"

Did he know what she'd been thinking? Rachelle wouldn't have had the courage. Or maybe now she would, all things considered, but she was still a little tongue-tied.

Amazingly, Eliska agreed. She retrieved her little purse, and they crossed the bridge to Old Town again, where she led them through the jumble of streets to a bar and restaurant that only the locals knew about, she said.

Over a lovely merlot they found they had other common interests, including, of all things, a mutual love of "Law and Order." When they realized they'd been laughing and chatting so long that dusk had fallen, they repaired inside, where Eliska insisted on ordering for them, speaking rapid-fire to the waiter without looking at a menu.

All during drinks and dinner, Eliska seemed to be flirting with them. Rachelle wondered if she was imagining it all, given her current mental state, but Eliska leaned toward her a lot, as well as toward Mike, and kept touching them, mostly Rachelle. Just little fingertip taps at first, when she was making a point. But then there were hands resting on knees, on shoulders, on thighs. Her gaze seemed open, frank, appreciating. When she invited them to her apartment, there seemed to be something laced in her words.

Either she had a murderous boyfriend back there who would dispose of their bodies when he was through with them, or she was actually coming on to them.

Rachelle decided she was willing to take the chance and find out.

They wound their way to Eliska's fourth-floor apartment, up creaking stairs to rooms filled with books and papers. She'd said she was getting her PhD, writing her thesis on porcelain production in Bohemia between 1918 and 1930.

It was ridiculous. Rachelle cradled her hands around the tiny espresso cup. It was too...right.

She'd told Eliska why they were here; about the cancer and the resultant promises she made to herself, not to evoke pity, but to explain. That had led to a spirited discussion of life goals and seizing the day and chasing dreams, and now they continued that theme.

"If I'm not mistaken," Eliska said, "you've never been one to limit yourself. Am I right?"

"I used to be," Rachelle said slowly. The wine and rich food had made her mellow, but the caffeine infused her with energy; she drifted somewhere between the two. "The cancer changed that."

Mike stood, brushed a kiss on her head. "Excuse me, ladies," he said, and headed to the bathroom.

Rachelle took a deep breath. Before she could say anything, however, Eliska said, "Forgive me if this is presumptuous, but the both of you...you're very attractive people."

"Thank you," Rachelle said. It sounded lame, but she felt a flush of pleasure at the compliment. And not just on her face.

"I hope you don't think I make a habit of picking up couples who come on my tours..." She laughed. "Oh, I'm sure I'm making a mess of things. But you two seem very open, and the way you're talking about embracing life... If I'm not picking up the signals I think I am, just put me out of my misery!"

Rachelle laughed and, acting on impulse, put her hand over Eliska's. "You're not misreading things, although please believe we're not in the habit of picking up our foreign tour guides, either!" Then, gathering every ounce of bravery, she added, "Just one in particular."

The best part, she decided later, was that they didn't have that awkward hesitation of deciding what to do next, or who should make the first move.

They both leaned in and kissed each other.

At first Rachelle found herself trying to compare it to her previous, muzzily remembered encounter, but soon she forgot all about that. She fell into sensations: soft lips, tentative kisses (who was supposed to be the aggressor?), the smell of some flowery perfume, and the taste of coffee on the breath of someone who was most definitely not her husband, the only person she'd kissed with this sort of intimacy in the past six years, which made it a different taste altogether.

The difference, and the femininity of the difference, thrilled her to her core.

A decidedly masculine clearing of a throat made them draw apart, reluctantly.

Rachelle stood and kissed Mike, thrilled with the familiarity of him and the familiar maleness of him. When they hugged, he said, for her ears only, "I love you."

And that was all that needed to be said.

Getting to the bedroom, slowly stripping each other of clothing—all of that was a blur, with snapshots and moments of memory that Rachelle captured for later.

Eliska undoing her hair, which tumbled heavily down her back.

Mike shrugging out of his shirt, but leaving on his pants for now, brushing his hand across the straining bulge in his crotch.

The press of Eliska's small, high breasts against her rib cage as Eliska reached behind Rachelle to unclasp her bra. The sparkle in Eliska's eyes as she did so, and the slow step backward so she could watch as the bra fell away. The feel of Eliska's cool fingers as she encircled Rachelle's full breasts, and the sound of her whisper: "Beautiful."

Although the rest of Eliska's apartment was simply furnished, her bed was a sumptuous four-poster with diaphanous fabric hanging from the rail and moving gently in the soft breeze from the open window. Rachelle fell, as if in slow motion, into the mound of feather pillows, laughing.

Then, not laughing, because what Eliska's lips were doing to the sensitive flesh of her neck was no laughing matter.

She squirmed, threading her hands through Eliska's lush hair and marveling at the feel of such a light, lithe body on top of her. Eliska rose up to plant kitten kisses on her mouth again, then headed farther south, trailing those light kisses down to Rachelle's breasts.

"Beautiful," she murmured again as she gathered them in her hands. She licked and nibbled, her tongue tiny and pointed, her touch excruciatingly delicate and direct. Rachelle squirmed, half-mad from the sensations that ignited a fire that trailed down to her clit and burned steadily brighter.

But she wanted more. She urged Eliska up so she could taste her pert breasts, relishing the feel of the budding nipples in her mouth, between her fingers. Eliska moaned, tossing her head. The sound enflamed Rachelle further.

She urged Eliska down against the mound of pillows and stroked her fingers along Eliska's thighs until Eliska parted them, whispering, "Oh, yes," when Rachelle leaned down.

Mike had been right, of course; Eliska did taste sweet and incredible, and Rachelle felt some sort of strange empowerment because she felt as if she knew, instinctively, what to do to drive Eliska's desire higher and higher: When to lick harder, when to back off. When to slip a finger inside and feel Eliska's inner walls clench.

She felt Mike's hands on her hips. He'd been there all along, stroking and caressing both of them, involved without being the focus. Now, she realized as if coming out of a dream, he was behind her.

He was naked.

He was hard, his cock once again teasing her slick lips, her swollen clit.

It was just like the other night after the bridge, she realized. It was pretty much the only thought she could hold in her head. Beyond that, there was only need: the need to bring Eliska to climax, to feel Mike explode inside of her, to come herself. Oh, god, yes. She was so close.

The delightful Eliska was writhing beneath her, and Rachelle wanted to feel her shudder and hear her cry out and taste her as she came.

Something else built up inside her as well. She was too hot, too on edge to step back and identify it, but she thought, fleetingly, that it had something to do with the moment: herself, on the brink of this new experience; Mike, always with her.

Then Eliska pitched over the edge of her own arousal, like a sweet gift. And Mike was moving inside of Rachelle, reaching around to flick against her clit, and she was breathing Eliska's scent, as she felt Eliska contract again and Mike's thrusts become a flurry, and Rachelle came.

* * *

Tomorrow they were heading to Budapest. Rachelle knew, in fact, that they couldn't spend the whole night in the comforting embrace of Eliska's featherbed...and Eliska, somehow curled around both of them. They needed to pack, to be at the train station early.

What she wanted, though, was to be awake at the first brush of dawn, to see the new day begin.

AN AGE PLAY

Regina Kammer

Αnd then he took her in his arms."

Every time I wrote those words, I swore I would never write them again. Yet they inexorably flowed from my fingers to the keyboard.

"And then he took her in his arms."

It was simply part of the romance novel formula: beautiful, virginal heroine with flowing locks and beseeching eyes falls for the extraordinarily handsome, charismatic—yet enigmatic—hero. Admittedly, it could be tiresome, except that I wrote for the Passion Flower imprint of Thorne Publishing. My characters got to have lots of sex, and I could make it as hot as I wanted, although nothing could be too shocking or my editor would chastise me later.

I let out a breath.

"Finished?" came my husband's voice from the next room.

I guess I had sighed pretty loudly. "Yes. The tropical island paradise was more challenging than I thought."

"Did he fuck her?" Mark leaned his lanky frame against the doorjamb, his salt-and-pepper curls in the usual tousled disarray.

"Not yet. Not until they're married. He pleasured her orally, though. Under a palm."

"So," he grinned teasingly. "Do you need to go downstairs?" He held out his hand.

I laughed. My husband knew me too well. I got up and threaded my fingers through his. "Yes," I smiled.

Like buoyant teens we walked from the office down the stairs to our bedroom.

"And who am I this time? A pirate?" he asked hopefully.

"No, dear, you're not a pirate." I casually took off my clothes.

"Why am I never a pirate? I want to be a pirate." He pulled off his sweatshirt.

"Maybe some day. Today you are an early nineteenth-century naturalist."

"That sounds a little nerdy for your readers, Jean, dear."

"He's hot—"

"Of course."

"—And he's on board an exploratory merchant ship to the South Seas. The widower captain of the ship has brought along his nineteen-year-old daughter."

"Why do they always have to be nineteen?"

"I could make her eighteen."

"Make her sixteen. Now that's hot."

"That's also kiddy porn according to Thorne. You know I have to be careful about that."

"Okay," he conceded. "But since I have to be a nerdy scientist, you have to be sixteen."

I laughed, surprised he wanted me to play at being that old.

I licked my lips and drew a finger down the middle of his chest, tangling the soft black and gray strands along the way. "Please be gentle, sir," I said with breathy anticipation, my timbre an octave higher than normal. "I've never been with a man before."

"Of course, my sweet." He kissed me hungrily as his hand skated gently along my curves. "What's your name?" he asked trailing kisses down my neck.

"Lily, sir."

"Ah, Lily, my innocent flower," he breathed softly. "I shall help you discover new pleasures." His fingers wandered over my belly to comb through the thatch of hair between my thighs. "Open your petals for me," he said mawkishly as he explored my silky flesh.

I was already sticky and swollen.

"You're as wet as a dewy field." His voice was deep, seductive.

"I don't understand, sir." I inhaled sharply when he began massaging my clit.

"You've never touched yourself?"

"No, sir, never," I said, naïveté tinged with a moan. I spread my legs to allow further invasion.

"You've never let one of your maidservants touch you?" His lips grazed my neck. "Caress you like this?"

His thumb was working my clit now, while two fingers slowly thrust inside me, keeping me on edge. I moved my hips against him encouragingly as he took me in a lusciously indulgent kiss.

He lifted my petite body and tossed me onto the bed. Feigning modesty, I scrambled under the sheets, which he promptly tore off. He shoved me back against the mattress and pushed my legs open with his knees, pressing his weight into my shoulders. His fully erect cock bobbed between us in anticipation. He smiled lasciviously.

I looked up at him with chaste yet beseeching eyes.

His fingers delved inside me once again, scooping up my moisture to lubricate his prick.

"You're still a virgin."

"Yes, sir," I whimpered.

He poised himself at the opening of my impatient cunt. "There may be a little pinch," he said darkly. "Trust me, it will feel wonderful in but a second."

He slammed into me, mercilessly burying himself to the hilt. I screamed and struggled under him.

"Please, sir! You're hurting me!" I was in ecstasy, my body pulsating around his demanding prick.

He grabbed my hands and pinned them over my head. "You love it, you little whore." He pumped in and out, his rhythm growing faster. "You lied. You've had men before."

"No, sir!" My body clenched around him. "Please...stop!" I was almost there.

His weight and strength held me captive against the bed. He was driving into me frantically, willing himself to climax.

"Who were they? Native boys? Or perhaps the ship's entire crew?"

"Yes!" I climaxed with a howling groan, squeezing him tightly, wanting his pleasure now. I rocked my pelvis to his time, clenching and releasing his pumping cock.

"How old did you say you were, Lily?" he panted.

I locked eyes with him. "I've just turned fifteen, sir."

"Fucking Christ!" He thrust his hips against mine and held himself there, his body spasming as he spent inside me.

With a thud and a moan, he crashed to the mattress. I glanced over at his sweaty smiling face.

"Not bad for a science nerd."

He chuckled and pulled me to him.

* * *

I never gave up my day job when I became an author. Once
I signed my publishing contract, I asked to be transferred to
"casual" status. After all, being a reference librarian at a university library positions me well for writing historical romances. If
I need to know about the cotton trade in 1820, I have a plethora
of resources right at my fingertips. Intellectually stimulating
with a flexible schedule—what more could I possibly want?

One typical Saturday, a rather attractive male student came
toward the information desk. I smiled. Tall, athletic, dark-
haired—he was the very image of one of my heroes.

"Jean?"

Once he spoke I knew who he was: the boy from my local
ballet studio. "Eric! I didn't recognize you with all your clothes
on," I joked.

That's dance class humor.

He grinned and blushed.

"I didn't know you worked here," he said shifting his weight
from one foot to the other. "I thought you were a writer, or
something."

"Well, I'm both." I couldn't stop smiling. I never realized
how cute he was, or how green his eyes were. "Aren't you a little
young for college?"

He chuckled. "I'm with my uncle." He pointed to a man my
age flipping through the student paper at the newspaper rack.
"He went here so he's showing me around. He wants me to
apply for next year."

"Stanford's pretty prestigious."

"Yeah," he agreed. "My parents're moving to Vermont," he
said, seemingly apropos of nothing.

"Oh. The winters will be rather different from California."

"Yeah," he laughed nervously. "So I figure I can go to college wherever I want since I have to move anyway." He drew abstract curves on the desk with a finger. "I've been thinking of Scotland. My mom's Canadian so, I think, it's, like, I can just go there, you know?"

God, I love the way teenagers talk.

"That's totally cool," I said in my own age-appropriate vernacular. "I'm taking a research trip to England next year."

His eyes brightened. "Nice." His uncle waved at him. "Gotta go. See ya."

I don't think I was too obvious as I watched him walk away. His dancer's butt looked good in fitted jeans.

The best thing about writing English Regency romances is the chance to actually travel to England under the guise of doing research and getting to write it off on our taxes. One of the joys of going with Mark was our playful reenactments of seduction scenes on location.

This time, though, work had prevented him from joining me.

"So...what are you wearing?" Mark asked sultrily over the phone.

"A shear cotton chemise with a drawstring neckline and pretty embroidered flowers."

"Really?" he said, breaking character. "Where'd you get that?"

"Some Jane Austen underwear shop. Yes, she's that popular."

Mark laughed. It was so good to hear his laugh even if he was six thousand miles away. I slunk further down into the mound of pillows on my bed. I was staying in an utterly quaint B&B in the even quainter town of Bath. It was easy to get into a romantic mood.

"Undo the bow at your neckline," he commanded. "And loosen the opening."

With one hand working my clothing and one hand playing between my legs, I did as I was told.

"Pinch your nipples." I did, even though they were already hard.

"Are you touching yourself?"

"Yes."

"Good," he murmured in satisfaction. "Are you wet?"

"Yes. Very."

I knew he was stroking himself, he didn't have to tell me.

"Are you alone?" he asked.

"No," I tantalized. "The gardener and butler are here, while the footmen stand guard. All eagerly await your instructions."

"Hmmm...one at a time? Or two at once?"

Either would do. "Yes, please." I bent my knees and dropped them open, my fingers delicately rubbing my engorged clit.

"The gardener...I want to watch that blond muscle boy come inside you," he said breathing heavily. "Spread his cheeks for me...I'll be on top fucking his tight ass."

Mark only talks like that when he's really horny. I smiled. He missed me. "Do you feel his huge cock inside you?" His voice was getting more and more ragged.

I really could have used my vibrator right about then. "Yes," I lied.

He sensed something was wrong. "Jean?"

"Hmmm?"

"Honey, I know you're not as far along as I am. What's going on?"

"I forgot to pack my vibrator. I'm a little slow to come without it."

"You remembered your hands-free but forgot your vibrator?"

"You would rather I had you on speaker-phone and got off more quickly?"

He laughed, a reaction overcome by his own masturbatory indulgence.

"So what are you using?" His heady tone indicated he was back to pumping himself.

"The handle of my hairbrush. Disappointingly inadequate."

"Intriguing," he said darkly. "Clearly I have failed to relieve you of all implements of self-deflowerment. You dare despoil yourself with a hairbrush, my virgin bride, and deny yourself the pleasures of a grown man's cock?"

The handle suddenly felt more gratifying.

"Perhaps I should have the strapping young bucks guarding your door hold you down while the butler and gardener take turns satisfying themselves in your unused cunt."

"Oh, yes, please." I was getting there. "I would like that very much."

"You little whore. I will take great pleasure in watching your defilement."

"Yes, sir—" I felt suspended above oblivion.

"I should have them both fuck you at once...one in your tasty little cunt...the other in your unyielding forbidden hole."

"Yes!" I gasped as a jolt coursed through my body, tingling my toes. "Come on me, sir. I want you to come on me while you watch."

"Oh, fuck!" he growled.

I could hear his satiated grunts over the phone. I smiled.

"Jean?"

"Yes, Mark?"

"I miss you."

For all the times I've been to England, oddly, for one who writes Regencies, I had never been to Bath. It is probably the most romantic town in that country, and there I was alone. Well, at least I would get more writing done than I usually do on my trips, and I could visit every single museum and historical site without complaint by my husband. I imagined all sorts of spousal reactions to my itinerary.

I was in the Costume Museum taking notes despite the dim lighting, when I saw a young man and woman holding hands. As I marveled to myself how the youth of England have interests far beyond their American counterparts, the boy looked at me and beamed.

"Hey, Jean! Fancy meeting you here!"

"Eric?" It took me a second to recognize him, what with the normal clothes and all. "I should say the same for you."

We hugged briefly. "I'm going to the University of Bath," he explained. "They have a really great performing arts department. And I figured the winters would be a little less cold in the south."

"I suppose so," I laughed.

"And you?"

"Research for my books."

"Let me introduce you to my girlfriend: Emma Boyle meet Jean Swan."

"Pleased to meet you, Emma." I stuck my hand out but the girl just stared at me, mouth open. Eventually, she shook my hand, still dumbfounded.

"You're Jean Swan? The Jean Swan?" She looked up at Eric. "You didn't tell me you knew Jean Swan!" She punched him playfully.

Okay, not dumbfounded; star-struck. It was so cute the way she said my name in her English accent.

"We were in ballet class together," Eric said sheepishly.

"I absolutely love your books," she gushed.

"Really?" I was genuinely astonished and pleased. "They're

aimed at middle-aged housewives, you know, not teenagers."

"My mum reads them, too."

Mum—that was so cute!

"Are you in town for long?" Eric asked keenly.

"Another two weeks or so. I'm using Bath as a home base to explore the area."

Emma looked at me wide-eyed.

I smiled. "For a whole series," I said to her.

"Are you by any chance free Friday night?" she inquired with marked enthusiasm while tugging on Eric's sleeve. "We all go to the Hare & Monk on Fridays."

They made a wonderful couple. I would have to include them in my next novel. "I would love to join you."

I had almost forgotten what it was like to be young, to constantly flirt in an atmosphere of sexually charged one-upmanship. I held my own quite remarkably, even making the boys blush, except Eric, who just laughed at my American vulgarity. The girls were simultaneously enchanted and enchanting. It turned out I was quite popular amongst college-aged female readers, at least those at the Hare & Monk, and eventually they garnered enough courage to interrogate me about how I write my salacious scenes. The boys pretended to tune out, but not very successfully.

We were there until closing time. The party was to continue at one of the boy's rooms. I begged out, knowing it would simply devolve into a snogging session. Eric chivalrously offered to walk me back to my B&B across town.

We took the sleepy streets lined with elegant stone town-houses, chatting mostly about Emma, me realizing I was tipsier than I thought I was, Eric steadying me a few times.

We strolled through the Royal Victoria Park along the Gravel Walk, avoiding furtive lovers in dark recesses. Catching a view of the Royal Crescent semi-ellipse bathed in light, I stopped. "Mark would really love this," I sighed.

Eric turned to me. "You miss him," he said nervously.

"Yeah."

I glanced up. His expression was filled with confusion and longing. We both quickly returned to staring at the architectural marvel before us.

And then he took me in his arms and kissed my open, surprised mouth.

Slow moving and drunk, I did not resist. Instead I melted in his embrace and let him devour me. God, he was a good kisser, and separated from Mark as I was for so long, I needed a good kissing.

Then guilt took hold of me and I pulled back a little. "Eric, what's going on?"

We remained touching cautiously, panting abashedly.

"I...I'm not sure," he stammered. "I'm completely in love with Emma. But she wants a romantic hero...I'm terrified I'll get it wrong. We're both virgins. All I've done is kiss some girls."

"Clearly."

He smiled at that. "I don't want to mess things up our first time, you know? I want it to be perfect." He looked in my eyes. "I need someone to show me what to do."

A chill of realization went up my spine. "You're suggesting I do that?"

"Ye-ah. Show me what girls want, what I'm supposed to do. Like what the guys in your books do."

Wow. "Look Eric, I'm supremely flattered, but you and Emma need to discover all that for yourselves."

"What if I do something wrong? Emma deserves the best."

"Eric, I'm married. I can't just go out and have sex with someone. Plus you're only seventeen—"

"I'm eighteen."

Well, that shot that line of reasoning down.

"I'm forty-two. Old enough to be your mother."

"You don't look or act like my mother."

Smooth. "Okay...still...I'm married. I'm in a monogamous committed relationship."

"He doesn't need to know. He's not here."

"Infidelity is not a lesson I want to teach you," I retorted. I turned my back to him, but he remained right there, moving closer, touching me on the shoulder with a featherlight caress, making me realize I was wet, startlingly so. Christ, this kid didn't need any lessons! "Eric, let me think about this. Please."

As he walked me back to my B&B, all I could think about was that he probably had an erection.

"We're here," I said when we reached the front gate.

"Jean, can I call you later this week? Do you have a mobile?"

We exchanged numbers, then he bent down and kissed me fleetingly before he left.

Inside my room, I was in a sexual frenzy. I couldn't call Mark; he'd still be at work. I masturbated thinking about Eric. I dreamt about him all night too, waking up sweaty and aroused. How could I possibly say no?

"Jean, something's wrong."

"Why do you say that?"

"We've been married for fifteen years. I know when something is bothering you."

I had to tell him. We'd been upfront and frank about everything: crushes, fantasies, possibilities.

"You remember that boy in my ballet class?"

"The kid with the butt?"

"Yeah. He's here, going to college. He has a girlfriend... they're both virgins. He wants her first time to be special. He wants someone to teach him how to have sex."

Silence.

"Mark? Are you there?"

There was an alarming pause before he answered, "Yes, I'm here."

I drew in a deep breath. "He wants me to be the one to teach him."

There. It was out.

"Shit."

"Mark—"

"I knew this would happen. We knew this would happen. It was just a matter of time." Mark exhaled long and hard. "You want to fuck him, don't you?"

"I don't know. I mean, I think so. I never thought about it before. No one's ever wanted to fuck me besides you since we've been married."

"That's not true. Matt does."

"Matt?" Shit. Matt was totally hot. Only a threesome would be hotter.

"And Sean."

"Please, Mark, don't tease me right now. Look, I'm alone. I write about sex all day. I forgot my vibrator. I've been propositioned by a very attractive young man whom I most likely will never see again. I'm being open and honest about what's going on."

I could almost hear his mind ruminating. "I guess I didn't expect to be this upset. And I always thought it would be me first."

"I don't have to."

"Yes you do." He paused, thinking again. "Jean," he said

finally. "Will this experience make you a better writer?"

"I hadn't thought of that," I conceded. "Maybe. Probably."

"Okay, then do what you feel you need to do. Honestly I can't say I'm truly happy about this, but I don't want to stop you either."

"I love you, Mark."

"I know."

Eric picked me up in what looked like an old Eurovan.

"When I got here in the summer I just found it easier to buy a car to get around," he explained nervously.

I knew how he felt; I had had butterflies since we made our date.

I hadn't thought about the logistics, but here he was with his van driving me to a secluded woody area just outside town. I didn't want to know what he told Emma he was doing that night.

He turned off the paved road and drove slowly down a path, the van bouncing suggestively. He stopped and parked. There was too much silence.

And while it had been his idea all along, I knew I would have to make the first move.

"Let's get comfortable in the back, Eric."

I write about seduction all the time, but this was just too surreal. Climbing onto the camping bed side by side was awkward. I felt his hands tremble when he dared to touch me. I reminded myself that I knew what I was doing. I pushed him onto his back, straddled him, and kissed him with all the passion I could muster.

That worked.

I felt his muscles tense excitedly under me, felt his instant erection through his jeans. He knew how to kiss, and the familiar action relaxed him. His fingertips danced across my back in a flustered rhythm.

"Unbutton my blouse," I said feigning confidence. "But don't take it off."

He did, with jittery hands.

I undid his fly and began pulling up his tucked-in shirt. I could feel him tense again, his breathing becoming irregular, stopping at times.

"Eric, has anyone ever, um, given you head before?"

He drew in a tremulous breath. "No."

He let me pull down his underwear and jeans partway, let me stroke him, let me wrap my lips and tongue around him, let me take him all the way to the back of my throat.

"Oh…my…god," he gasped.

He was huge and amazingly hard. He was also young and came almost instantly in my mouth.

"I'm sorry," he apologized sincerely, still twitching from my ministrations.

"I wanted you to do exactly that." I climbed up to meet his face. "I want you to last a little longer when we—you know."

In the dim moonlight I could see him smile.

"So have you ever seen a woman's"—god, what did kids say? "Hoo-ha?"

He licked his lips. "No."

"Not even porn?"

"Well, okay, I mean, sort of. But never in real life."

"Do you have a flashlight?"

"You mean a *torch?*" he teased retrieving one from the glove box.

I made him take off my cords and panties—he'd have to learn, right? I spread my legs and shone the light onto my privates.

He bit his lower lip and his eyes widened as I gave my erotic lesson. He listened, engrossed, touched and stroked eagerly, licked and fingered enthusiastically. My orgasm was proof that he was a very good student.

We lay side by side, kissing and fondling gingerly. "What does it feel like for girls...for you?" he asked.

"Probably the same as for boys: building up to a peak, simultaneously wanting and not wanting to reach that peak, an explosion in both mind and body, then a feeling of warm relaxation."

He picked at the lace of my bra.

"Take it off," I said.

He was nervous again, and his clammy fingers worked the plastic front closure clumsily with little success.

Although disheveled and unfastened, he was fully clothed. I took control, pulling everything off him, purposely tickling him in the process, until he lay on his back nude, laughing, and, most importantly, relaxed.

In the sensual melee, he had managed to get everything off me as well.

It was time; we both knew it. He had brought condoms. I hadn't used a condom for years, but luckily they're pretty much the same as they always were.

"The other way," I said. "You'll know, 'cause it rolls down easier."

His cock was magnificent, its size contrasting sharply with his skinny, still-boyish, almost hairless body. I touched his cheek, realizing he probably only had to shave a couple of times a week. And yet, despite his youth, he exuded a raw masculine sexuality.

"I want you, Eric." I leaned back and arranged my legs on either side of him. He remained kneeling, afraid but still erect.

I nudged him down. "Use your hands to guide yourself."

He hesitated.

"I'll help." I realized at that moment how desperate I was for him.

He sighed as he entered me, slowly pushing deeper, until he was fully enveloped by my warmth. He stayed there, breathing heavily, possibly unsure what to do next.

"Move in and out—"

"I know—I think. I'm just surprised. This is incredible."

I smiled and pulled his face to mine, kissed him and moved my hips encouragingly.

God, his thick cock felt good inside me. I could hold off my orgasm no longer. I felt the wave overtake me as I clenched him powerfully.

It was his undoing.

Eric gulped for air as his hips jerked against mine. He stayed frozen, hovering over me, his mouth open, still uttering choking sounds. Suddenly, he exhaled, and his weakened body slumped against mine.

"Oh, my god," he said. "I never...I didn't..." he trailed off. His heart thumped loudly as he tried to steady his breathing.

It was a most satisfying beginning to a long night of discovery for both of us.

The next spring's offerings by the Passion Flower imprint of Thorne Publishing included *The Widowed Countess,* the story of Emma, the twenty-eight-year-old Countess of Boylestone, who falls in forbidden love with her eighteen-year-old footman, taking his virginity and unleashing his sexual desires. Unbeknownst to her, he is the illegitimate son yet ultimate heir of her dead husband's business partner, the Earl of Bathampton.

"I wanted to make her older, like thirty-five," I explained to Mark as he paged through my advance copy.

"So why didn't you?"

"My editor thought it would be gross. Like when she's fifty he'd only be in his early thirties. That's too kinky for Thorne."

"And how is it that a raven-haired, emerald-eyed, awesomely-buffed eighteen-year-old is still a virgin?"

"His father instills in him a sense of honor and pride. Farm girls and servants are not good enough. So when the beautiful countess seduces him, he is totally ready."

Thorne initially was not sure their market would go for such a story, but within a week of the release, they were proved wrong. It shot to number one on their bestseller list.

Knowing Emma Boyle in Bath would eventually get a copy, I left a veiled note for her boyfriend on the acknowledgments page:

Dedicated to my loving husband, and a certain young man. He knows who he is.

ARE YOU SURE?

Alexander Liboiron

Are you sure?"

"About what?"

"Are you sure you want to do this?" she asked for the third time.

"Yes, I am." He didn't sound nearly as nervous as she felt, probably because he had never done it before. "What are you worried about?"

"We don't have to, I don't want to weird you out." She hated this part, when she wanted to back out, but the conversations, the revelations about personal fantasy, the dares and the insinuations had finally gone too far. It was amazing how you could love someone, and know they loved you, and still be worried about revealing something to them. She knew she was committed. "I have had guys try this and then decide it was too strange."

"Stop. Enough of that," he said, and silenced her by putting his hand on her throat. The pressure on her collarbone arrested her, his fingers firmly on her left shoulder, his thumb in the soft crevice below her neck. She could feel her pulse through his hand and wondered how he felt about her sudden intake of breath. Was he surprised? Did he notice how the irises of her eyes dilated, how her hands unclenched reflexively? Certainly he noticed how her chin lifted up, lengthening her neck.

He seemed to take the motion in stride. He easily moved into her, pressing her against the wall with his body. It didn't seem forced or awkward, which she had experienced with past lovers. The motion seemed natural to him, an expression of a genuine desire, rather than just a thing done to satisfy her fantasies.

She didn't realize her lips were parted until he kissed her, first gently, then forcefully. She savored the feeling of being able to strain slightly against him, to struggle against his grip on her neck and the force of his form pressing into hers. As she strained against him, she felt him return her pressure. He matched and easily exceeded her strength, and she felt, just for a moment, the languorous ability to push against him as much as she was able and still feel herself contained.

Then he released her, and she fell forward against his chest gasping. "How was that? Was it what you were looking for?"

She smiled and caught her breath. "That was...ah, that was good. I liked that," she said. "Let's do that some more." She began to head nervously for her bedroom. The rush had left her, and she hoped that he would be willing to continue. Too often neck-grabbing would be the end of it.

She wanted more.

Her collection of toys was eclectic. It ranged from things that any girl could be expected to own: dildos, paddles, vibrators, things he was already familiar with. She went past those and into the storage boxes she had never shown him, usually kept under the bed. She pulled them out one by one—the riding crop, the wrist and ankle cuffs, the opera gloves, the gags—watching his face, waiting for the cringe. She was proud of her leather and chain collection, but always in private.

His face was carefully neutral. He picked up a gag, one of her favorites, with a panel to go over her mouth and a leather ball attached to the inside. He looked at it clinically.

"So, you want me to tie you up, tightly, with all of this," he gestured at the ropes and leather cuffs, "and then you want me to torture you. And then you want me to hit you and fuck you. Quite hard, harder than you think I will feel comfortable with." He looked her in the eye, apparently unperturbed.

"Before we get started," she said. "I want to make sure you understand why." She swallowed and paused, trying to find the right words in her anxiety. "It's more about 'how,' really. Don't treat me as though I'm a naughty child, or a bad girl, or being punished, well, maybe we can do 'punished' some other time." She was getting ahead of herself. "I don't want to feel that I'm bad or wrong or wicked. I don't want you to hit me because I deserve it."

He thought for a moment. "Why do you want me to hit you?

"Hit me because I want you to." She swallowed. "Hit me because it feels good and makes me want to come."

"Okay," he said after another pause, and her heart sank. He didn't get it. This was too far past the typical naughty play. She got ready for the first unsatisfying touch, the too timid slap or spank that would show his hidden discomfort. She had been here before; schoolgirl role-playing was fun, but it didn't go where she wanted to go. When it was over and done, the fantasy was finished and everyone could put his kink away safely in a drawer until the next time. It was as if they were saying, "You're not naughty anymore, so I won't hit you."

She had learned from experience, though, that her kink

wouldn't go away. She didn't want the bondage or the play to stop just because she took off a plaid skirt. She always wanted more, and that freaked men out. They didn't have the energy to maintain the control she ultimately wanted.

"Okay, so you want me to tie you up, fuck you and hit you like I mean it." Was he smiling?

"Yes."

He slipped the gag into her mouth and tied it tightly around her head. Her jaw responded with the familiar ache, and the leather ball in her mouth choked off any further reply.

"Are you sure?" He was definitely smiling. She nodded

She had planned an explanation for each toy, how it was used, how she liked it used. With the gag securely in place, her voice had been taken from her. So she stood mutely as he lifted the bottom of her shirt over her stomach, grazing his fingers across her skin as he went. She felt his fingernails trail across her bra and he raised her arms above her head and pulled her shirt over her eyes. He stopped there for a moment and held her wrists in one hand, tightly. He pulled her arms so her spine arched backward and guided her, staggering, toward the bed. Unhooking her bra, he lifted it over her shoulders and tossed both it and her shirt aside.

She felt naked with him now, though she still wore a skirt, more than she ever had before. Seeing her gagged and topless was seeing her desires exposed and she felt vulnerable and raw, as if her skin was tender and would easily bruise. She was aware that she was panting around the gag. He turned her around, roughly forced her to her knees and put the cuffs on her wrists, linking them together with the same lock he used to fasten them. The flesh side of the leather cuffs felt warm and smooth against her skin, and the click of the lock sent a small shiver up her arms. With her hands bound behind her back he bent her forward, over the bed. A chill ran up her spine as her skin pebbled in anticipation of what she hoped would come. Her erect nipples pressed into the sheets, and she felt the texture of the fabric rub against them.

He grabbed her hips tightly, as if he was preparing to enter her from behind. He gripped the waistband of her skirt, caught it and her panties under his fingers and pulled them down her thighs to the floor.

"Lift your knees, one at a time, starting with the right." His voice was softer than she expected it to be and nearer her ear. She did as she was told, relishing the chance to obey an order. She felt herself becoming wet, and she allowed herself to have high hopes. This was going very well. She lifted one leg slightly, then the other, as he pulled her skirt off. He didn't tease or take his time; he used quick, confident motions. Had this been a fantasy of his as well? Or did he have experience with a previous lover?

She felt him slide the ankle cuffs over her feet, tighten them securely and then lock them. Once again the action of the lock fastening made an audible *click* and sent a shiver up her legs, this one reaching all the way to her clitoris. She wondered how she looked from behind—were her pussy lips red? Was she visibly wet? She hoped she was, hoped that her arousal was visible, that nothing about her was hidden from him. She felt more and more naked, less and less in control, and the thought of not knowing what was next made her moan softly, a sound not quite stifled by the gag.

She thought she heard him laugh. Was he aroused? Was he erect? Would he take her from behind while she was helpless to resist? Not that she would, but it was exciting to know that she had no options.

His hands were on her neck again, and his weight on her

back caused her to take short, shallow breaths. He grabbed her hair firmly in his fist and pulled back on it, lifting her head off of the bed as he placed a collar beneath her neck. It was tall and made of stiff leather, a posture collar she had bought but had been too nervous to wear during sex. It was just a little too restrictive, and she was surprised he had selected it. And pleased. She had hoped he would be willing to push her just a little, to take her just one step past her own boundaries.

She began to grind her hips into the edge of the bed. As he released her hair, she craned her neck, eager to feel the collar tight around her neck. She felt him pull it taut, felt it lift her chin and sink down against her collarbone, felt it wrap around her, encircling her throat. She closed her eyes and savored the feeling of being tied up, being helpless and bound.

She didn't expect the pain. It sent a shock through her and startled her so completely that at first she wasn't sure of its source. She wanted to curl up, but the collar and the cuffs kept her rigid. A sound came to her, the pleasant clap of a paddle, and she realized she had just been spanked. He hadn't taken the time to warm her up or to start softly, asking, "Is this good?" or asking which paddle she liked. He hit her again, even harder. The pain radiated up her back and down her legs and became something altogether more than pain in her crotch. He hit her once more, and then again in rapid succession, and she felt her whole body quake with each strike.

When he paused she pushed backward, thrusting her ass out to him, begging him with her body to continue. She tried to look back, but the collar kept her eyes fixed forward. Instead of pain, though, she was rewarded with the feeling of his fingers on her crotch. He touched her lips gently, carefully avoiding her clitoris, teasing her. He slowly spread her lips apart with two fingers and with a third gently stroked her, careful not to actually penetrate her. She could tell that she was getting his fingers wet. He was spreading her open, looking at and into her, getting his fingers wet with her. She clenched her pussy, hoping that he would fill it soon.

Instead, he spanked her again, striking not only her asscheeks but also her protruding, thrusting labia, shocking her and making her arch forward again. She cried out in pain and surprise and felt her eyes water. Twice more he hit her before she heard him set the paddle down on a chair. The pain and the pleasure and the surprise had brought her to a place where the only sound she could make was a low, continuous moan, and once again she began rubbing her hips into the edge of the bed.

She felt something wet and slick and realized he was rubbing lube into her crotch. Finally, he was going to take her. She closed her eyes. Instead, she felt his finger on her ass, rubbing lube into it, pushing her open and sliding his finger into it. He was incremental with the penetration and clearly had experience with anal play. Fist, he played with one finger, until he could bring it up to the final knuckle. He switched to two, playfully spreading her anus until it began to hurt just a little, then relaxing his motions, gently training her body to do what he wanted. She kept up her moan, punctuated by sharper cries and lower groans as he teased her and played with her.

At last she felt him press something hard into her asshole, felt the roundness of it spreading and opening her. She hoped it was his dick and pushed her ass back, hoping to fill herself with him. The pressure built and then quickly dropped off, and she realized he was pushing her anal beads into her, one after another in slow succession. The disappointment turned to anticipation. He wasn't done with her yet.

She ground her hips into the bed again and began to suck

on the ball in her mouth. Her body began to tremble, and she clenched her ass muscles around the beads. Reading her suddenly jerky motions, he slipped one finger into her pussy, and the feeling of his finger inside her caused her entire body to pulse tremulously with a small orgasm. She felt it build inside her, start to multiply.

Then he pulled his finger out.

"Not yet," he said into her ear. She felt the command sink into her body, felt herself go stiff and still, trying to prevent any further arousal. It felt so good to have him deny her something she so wanted, to allow his words to constrain her. She breathed slowly, feeling herself come back from the edge.

She didn't realize he was naked until she felt his penis touch her ass. She held her breath, her jaw aching, hoping that he would fill her. She felt the head of his penis push against her lips, felt his hands on her hips, felt herself slightly, tantalizingly parted. Her groaning was replaced by panting and then by whimpers. *Fuck me, please, open me and take me and make me yours and...*

His first, slow thrust interrupted her. He pushed the head of his penis into her and then paused, enjoying her restrained efforts to pull him more deeply into her. She clenched with her pussy and pushed her body back, but he wouldn't let her hurry him. He eased himself into her slowly, so that she could feel when the head of his penis pushed past her lips. He pushed gradually until his pelvis was resting against her asscheeks. Then he pushed a little more, crushing himself into her, and in the process thrusting against the base of the anal beads, so that he seemed to fill both holes at once. She cried out, stiffening her back, clenching and unclenching her hands in a futile effort to reach him and grab him and pull him even deeper.

He began to fuck her steadily, slowly pulling himself out

of her and then firmly pressing back in, gradually increasing the tempo. She met him at every thrust, desperately trying to pull him deeper into her. The invasion of the anal beads and his penis at the same time and the ball gag in her mouth made her feel deliciously full, overfull yet wanting more. His rhythm increased, and she felt her body tremble at each gentle impact, her skin move and tighten, her nipples slide against the sheets. She was wet and open and filled and bound, and straining against the bindings only made her pulse pound faster and her breath come shorter.

She could hear him panting and straining against her body, and the sound of him fucking her made her eyes roll back. She felt his fingers tighten and his pace became more frantic. He wanted her and had taken her and had bound her. He had denied her a voice and had hit her, and everything began to meld together—the tightness of the beads in her ass and the ache of her jaw around the ball and the steady pounding of his hips and his penis thrusting into her—and she came powerfully, her entire body coiling tight and loosening, and with each release came an orgasm and a scream so loud the gag couldn't dampen it.

Each orgasm led to the next, and they chained together for what seemed like hours, each one making her shudder, until the sheets beneath her face were wet from tears and the sheets beneath her crotch were soaked. Still he kept on and as her orgasms faded, she relaxed into the pleasure of him using her, past when she was done, to satisfy himself. At last he came into her, filling her completely, and lingered inside her. She could feel his penis softening inside her vagina and could feel her muscles slowly relax.

At last he pulled out, and the sensation of emptiness he left behind was only eased as he leaned forward, putting his weight on top of her, and wrapped his arms around her, encircling her waist and holding her breasts. She could feel him breathing heavily, his chest rising and falling in time with hers.

"There are a lot of toys you have here that we didn't get to," he whispered softly. She smiled—it was as good as a promise to do this again and soon.

JENNA'S
GAMBIT

Jeremy Edwards

There was no doubt that Jenna liked the way this felt. The dully aching clench in her groin was pleasurable rather than painful, and the tickle of not-quite-urgent need felt downright delicious when she squeezed her thighs together.

In fact, poised here on her bar stool, Jenna found that her only discomfort was psychological: would she have the nerve to go through with this?

She'd planned the entire evening around it, she told herself, glancing at the two empty beer bottles in front of her. By focusing on her emotional investment in tonight's gambit, she managed to provoke a surge of confidence. A shiver of erotic anticipation came in tow.

She was wise enough to act at this juncture, while the confidence was surging. In any event, it wasn't the only thing that was surging; she couldn't wait much longer.

"Can we go home now?" She put her hand on Eric's knee. "I'm horny," she whispered. It was the truth, if not the whole truth.

Eric grinned. Without articulating an answer, he stood up and reclaimed his denim jacket from the back of his stool. For an instant, Jenna thought she noticed his eyes drifting toward the rear of the restaurant, where two restroom doors straddled a "staff only" passageway.

She dismounted and insinuated herself into the crook of his arm, letting her chest warm his frame. The smell of his skin reminded her that this was a man who had long ago accepted her, 100 percent, for who she was. He was crazy about 90 percent of it and okay with the rest.

Nothing bad was going to happen tonight.

"I love you," she murmured into his throat. Her pelvis gyrated in slow motion.

Just nine blocks more, she told herself as they walked, hand in hand. *Just seven more blocks...six...* For a second or two around block five, she thought she might not make it—not because of miscalculation, but because of arousal. But she reasserted control, and the tickle felt better than ever. Soon the fence was in sight.

They'd stopped at this safe little neighborhood park before, on other nights when they'd been out for drinks. Eric would always wait at the gate while Jenna dashed in to water the ground.

On one occasion it had been Eric who'd requested a moment among the trees, and Jenna had stood on the sidewalk watching a crescent moon sail in and out of clouds, while she strained her ears for the distant sound of her lover's tight, male stream of release. Her pussy had sweetened with slickness as she listened.

"I need to stop at the park," she said tonight, as they approached it. She could detect the tremble of excitement—and nervousness—in her own voice. She observed with approval that dusk still lingered on this lazy June evening, offering reasonably good visibility for anyone who had something bold and compelling to look at. She'd counted on this.

"See you in a minute," said Eric, pulling her toward him for what he obviously expected to be a quick, affectionate peck on the lips.

But Jenna didn't let go. Instead, she pressed herself against the front of Eric's jeans and kept her mouth as close to his as she could without impairing speech. Her clit buzzed as the friction from Eric's crotch complemented the giddy tease of holding on just a little longer.

"I want you to watch me."

The admission, though softly spoken, resonated deeply in the quiet of the night.

She was heartened to note—proud, even—that at this critical moment it was not her anxiety that came to the fore, but her joy: her sensuous relishing of an act that for her held no shame, except insofar as it had always seemed a shame not to share such an intense and intimate area of pleasure with the man she loved.

In the instant that she waited for his response, a tide of memories welled up—like the water inside her; memories of the times she'd brought herself off on the seat while she did it, imagining that she had an eager male audience.

She recalled the workdays where she'd kept herself right on the edge as long as possible at her desk, fidgeting and fantasizing, until she was an inch away from rubbing her pussy in a frenzy—and a breath away from soaking herself.

She remembered those nature hikes with women friends during college—how the other gals had perennially been concerned that some guy might come along just when they were squatting, bare-bottomed, to make their girly rivulets...and how Jenna, by contrast, had secretly hoped for such an eventuality.

Eric's eyes were alive with interest, beneath asymmetrically cocked brows. "Well, then," he said with a reassuring jauntiness. "Lead the way."

Jenna sighed, basking in the good vibes of his complicity. It was really happening. She pressed a hand to where her body readied for release.

They shuffled together shyly, like virgins, to the dense bank of trees. When they arrived, she hugged him again.

He laughed. "I thought you had to go."

She ground into him. "I do, I do. Fuck, I'm nearly wetting my panties." It thrilled her to say it aloud—*wetting my panties*—and once again she wondered if he had any idea how raunchy she was, deep inside her private world, on this hitherto unbroached subject. "But I'm so turned on knowing that I'm going to"—she hesitated only a fraction of a second over the word—"pee in front of you." She savored the magic of the situation before finally breaking away from him to lift her skirt.

She held the miniskirt in folds just above crotch level, clutching fabric and self in one handful, pushing her mound against manic fingers while she feasted on the exhilaration of display. She was almost reluctant to stop fondling herself long enough to get her pussy out in the open.

Eric was staring at her with fascination, a hand grazing a ridge in his jeans.

"Well?" he prompted sweetly, but with an undercurrent of urgency. "Let's see you take those panties down and make a pretty puddle, gorgeous."

She hadn't been prepared for the possibility that Eric would be so wrapped up in the show she was staging, right away. The sense of gratification that washed through her was overpowering.

As she hooked the fingers of her free hand into the waistband of her lime bikini briefs, "pretty puddle" rang like the sexiest poetry.

"You're going to do it right from between your legs, aren't you?" he asked rhetorically. "Nothing like how a boy does it, eh?" He seemed to know exactly what she wanted to hear—as if she'd tape-recorded the fantasies in her head, and he'd been rehearsing from the transcripts.

She moaned in lieu of a reply, and Eric licked his lips while she scrunched her panties out of the way and bent her knees. She saw his gaze go appreciatively to the smooth roundness of her exposed ass.

"Come on," he said, with gentle insistence. "Show me what a woman you are. Show me how you pee, Jenn."

The words might have looked silly on paper, but in the night air they pinged Jenna's nipples and made her clit throb. As she felt the first tentative drizzle of piss blazing a trail down her slit, she couldn't recall ever being so turned on.

She ached with visceral bliss as her muscles creaked open and the hot trickle kissed her pussy lips on its way to lower ground. She used her hand to coax the engorged lips farther apart, while the knowledge that Eric was watching her every action thundered in her consciousness.

Oh, yes, she'd gotten herself exquisitely aroused by curating those beers all this while. But letting go of them at last was positively heavenly. It felt so good that her eyes blinked closed and her shoulder blades quivered. And when the flood began in earnest as her muscles twanged back into relaxation and freedom, Jenna squealed with raw delight.

Oh, it felt so good, so good. She let her fingers brave the downpour to skitter along her sex.

She opened her eyes to find Eric's attention locked on the feminine wall of water that rushed from her underside, cascading to earth with all the ecstatic turmoil of an impassioned lover. She fantasized, without even meaning to, that the whole neighborhood could hear her pissing—and she embraced the image.

She felt so lewd and fulfilled and desirable and honest, peeing her heart out for her man. She felt she was a living expression of natural womanliness and lust, with a river of love and libido pouring from between her thighs.

Her forefinger was riding her clit, and now she was coming. Her legs were twitching and all her nerves were crackling, each neuron individually intoxicated and euphoric. Her pussy was the center of the universe, and the muscles she peed with spasmed in satisfaction as the final drips and drops luxuriated out of her.

Jenna and Eric remained silent, in a kinky afterglow, while she reached in her skirt pocket for tissues. Eric stroked his fly as he watched her wipe her pussy, thigh flesh and fingers. It was quickly done, and yet she didn't change positions when the task was accomplished.

Except to step out of her panties.

Her eyes met his.

He was behind her with unzipped jeans in a heartbeat, encircling her waist and aligning their bodies.

"That was magnificent," he slurred in her ear, as if drunk on her spectacle. He slapped her right asscheek lightly, then groped her there until she jiggled. He teased the soft pout of her vulva, and she widened her stance farther, elevating her derriere and leaning forward to brace herself on a tree trunk.

The collegial horniness of his bloated cock, sliding lusciously into her, underscored the fact that she had made Eric wild by peeing for him. Inside her fuck-hungry cunt, this evidence of her effect on him sparked a network of sensations that spread in all directions to delight her—just as the orchestrated paradise of orgasmic, exhibitionistic release had rocked her body a few minutes earlier.

He began pounding in and out. Each inward thrust, like an accented syllable, hammered home what she'd done here tonight. "I *peed*, I *peed*, I *peed*," sang her inner voice, in time with the rhythm. "I fucking *peeeeeeeed*," said her new orgasm, the *e*'s trickling out like more pee, to be heard as a beautiful shriek in the twilight. The sound made Eric wiggle inside her like an out-of-control screwdriver. He came with a carnal sob.

"I have to piss like a son of a bitch now," he informed her after he had pulled out and she'd danced back into the panties. He touched her elbow. "Does that make you excited, you little tinkle-angel? To think about my warm cock all set to piss and piss while you look?" He chuckled when she nodded through hot blushes.

She watched him take his semiflaccid pink flesh in hand; she got an excellent view when he turned in profile to aim at a tree.

She shoved two fingers into her mouth as she admired Eric's stately arc. When she sucked, rocking in place, she tasted the salty tang of a stray, lingering drop of her own.

Still leaking, Eric growled, a satisfied animal—"*Ahhh*"—and Jenna tried to imagine precisely what it felt like for him to let pleasure stream and stream through his dick while he emptied. Her own groin muscles flexed idly in sympathy, and the delectable wetness of renewed want licked into her clinging panties.

He winked at her as he zipped up. The night was turning pleasantly breezy, and Jenna heard the wide-open park gate knocking against the fence: gate and fence banged like a pair of happy fuckers.

Eric took her hand. "I don't know about you, but I'll be ready for another beer when we get home."

His palm, squeezed against hers, was solid like a promise.

THE FEMALE
GAZE

Rachel Kramer Bussel

Ever since they'd started dating three years before, Alex had
been telling Rory about the boys who hit on him—the men,
the bears, the daddies, the silver foxes; the ones who looked
like they were barely legal, the shy boys who found in him
a kinship, or just a look, a lust, an impulse. "The bartender
comped my drink, then slipped me his number. Do I have to
put on a wedding band before they get the picture?" he'd ask,
chuckling as he kissed her lightly.

She ran her hands through his thick black hair before telling
him that a wedding ring had never been a deterrent to men
hooking up with other men. Maybe she should have been
bothered by people checking out her man, who'd once been a
model and graced ads for Calvin Klein underwear and Brooks
Brothers before deciding that he really preferred environmental
law. But she didn't mind, not really, and she certainly didn't
begrudge these men their hungry stares, their heartfelt offers.
The women she could do without, the ones who blatantly

clocked her man while they walked down the street, the ones who she could tell would take her husband into the bathroom for a quickie if they thought they could get away with it. Rory wasn't sure why, exactly, the former amused her and the latter annoyed her, but there it was. Actually, it was more than that; the thought of these men kissing her boyfriend; running their hands all over his firm, muscular body; swallowing his cock; plundering his bottom as she'd only fantasized about doing; well, it turned her on.

She couldn't help but wonder if they saw in Alex the same things she did. Was that possible? Were they clairvoyant—or just horny? Was he just another pretty face or did they want him to speak to them in that booming, low voice? Did they want him to order them around, like he ordered her? "Touch yourself for me. Show me how wet you are. Fuck yourself with the vibrator I got you." Would Alex be a top or a bottom in bed with a man? The more these men propositioned him, the more Rory found these naughty images creeping into her mind when she was alone, when she let her fingers wander between her lips and her mind go free.

Alex had beautiful olive skin and intense brown eyes and was strong in ways she was still coming to understand three years into their relationship. He was stubborn, yet she could melt him with a single, sensual smile, with a nip of her teeth against his arm, with a lick of her tongue along the center of his palm. She'd been known to interrupt him in the kitchen, where he did most of the cooking, to simply get on her knees and worship his enormous, beautiful cock. It was not only long, it was fat, wide around. She'd taken him between her lips countless times, in six states and three countries. His perfect cock had been in her ass twice, two of her favorite memories of their time together. He didn't mind her occasional petulance, and she forgave him his stubborn meltdowns, because everything else was so electric.

Nothing was missing between them, on the surface, at least, and yet she wanted something more. She surveyed her own boyish body in the mirror, staring at the freckles dotting her face, the small B-cup breasts, the tiny pooch of her belly and her small torso. She was boyish, but she was no boy. She had an ass, one that Alex loved to slap and beat with one of the many toys they kept for just such a purpose. He loved how wet she got when he held her throat tight while she struggled to get away, but not really. In turn, Rory loved that side of him, the one she thought of as manly. All too often she was called a dyke, or had been assumed by guys she went out with to be some kind of goth punk bitch goddess who wanted to slap them around, based on her short hair and layers of black and silver. She didn't necessarily mind either assumption—she'd bedded her share of girls, boyish like her, and curvy lipsticked lasses, and she could be tough when she wanted to be. She wasn't a top, not really... but she could still see Alex on the bottom.

She shut her eyes and stood there, naked, asking herself what she was looking for. Not another man—at least, not one for her. Alex was her soul mate; that much was clear. But she did have these dreams that wouldn't go away, flashes of Alex naked, bound, his mouth open, his body bared...for another man, one bigger and stronger than him, one who could make him beg and whimper the way he made her beg and whimper, strain and arch, scream and cry, in bed.

Who knows if she'd have thought of it on her own if Alex hadn't planted the seed, over and over. He liked to joke about it, but she could tell that somewhere inside he was flattered by the attention. Girls fawning over him could mean they wanted the status of being seen on his arm, a glamorous dinner or a ring on their finger. He'd made it clear those weren't the kinds of girls he wanted; she'd seen him point her out to some hopeful busty blonde, seen their eyes narrow as they took in her appearance, her clear defiance of what a pretty girl should look like.

But the men were something else, and she wanted to know what that something was. Who would Alex be when the boy/girl equation was stripped away, when it was simply pure testosterone thrown together? Well, pure testosterone and her. She didn't believe in the strictness of sexual orientation, the way men wrapped their heterosexuality around themselves so tightly they could barely smile at another man, nor in the halfhearted female bi-curiosity shown on any given night at any nightclub—or reality show—in America. She wanted to find out what might happen when all bets were off, and not just secondhand. She wasn't really into girls, not the way she was into Alex, not in a forever kind of way, but she knew what it was to fall to her knees in awe over a woman who simply knocked her out, whether the big, quiet butch at her gym, the one who seemed to fuck her simply by raking her eyes down Rory's body, or the Indian exchange student whose waist-length black hair smelled like flowers, who had kissed Rory dizzy.

She didn't know what to expect, but she knew she had to try, not just for her sake, or Alex's, but for their relationship, for the future. She didn't want to suddenly be a middle-aged wife who'd passed up the chance to live out a fantasy and then regretted it. She wanted to see, to watch, to know not by doing, but by seeing, by living vicariously; there, but not there, an outsider whose orchestration would let the two men be insiders.

One Wednesday night, Alex came home late, slipping into bed next to her, where she was flicking through channels aimlessly. "It happened again," he said, chuckling and reaching beneath her nightshirt for her nipple. "The pizza delivery guy, of all people. He told me to put his tip in his pants."

She couldn't help laughing at that, even as her nipple hardened while she pictured Alex's hand wrapping around the faceless guy's cock. "What if you said yes?" she asked before she could stop the words.

"To the pizza guy? I think I'd smell like pizza." He laughed, but as clichéd as that image was, Rory didn't. Just then, more than anything, she wanted to see him with another man, any man, really...well, any man who Alex showed a hint of desire for. She didn't want him to do it for her, exactly, but for them.

"But what if...I was there?" she asked as she writhed against him, pulling her body away from him so her trapped nipple was stretched, flattened. "What if I watched you two, and you could watch me? What if I touched myself while it happened?"

"Rory, what are you talking about? I mean, nothing against gay guys but...I'm not one. You know that," he said as he pulled her close, his hard cock burrowing between her legs. He let go of her nipple and grabbed his dick to press it against the rosebud of her ass, a place he'd only gone those two times before. Was he saying that he wanted to fuck another guy there? Or that he wanted her to be quiet, to focus on him and only him?

"I'm not saying you're gay, baby," she said, because lord knew he loved every inch of her body, overwhelmingly, voraciously. "But...there are shades of gay, shades of want that maybe you'll discover. I don't want you to do anything you don't want to do—I wouldn't enjoy that—but maybe there's something to all those guys approaching you, maybe it means something you can't truly understand until you act on it."

"I'll give you that," he said as he played with her clit, still nudging her ass—she could tell he was probably going to make her beg to be fucked there, if she truly wanted it, just because he could, because it was such a rarity—as his fingers made her open to him. "But what am I supposed to do, just go home with the next guy who offers? I don't want to do anything without you. We tried that and you know how I felt." She did. For a little while, they'd tried to have a totally open relationship and had picked up partners with all the enthusiasm of the sexually liberated, only to find that, once chosen, those partners seemed to lose much of their appeal after they'd gotten naked with them. Something was missing, and the only truly satisfying extracurricular sexing they'd done had happened with them and another woman.

"No, that's not what I'm saying. I guess I just want us to try this. I can't really say why but...it makes me very, very wet." His fingers pressed inside her to find out just how true that statement was, and she pressed down against him. "And I have this hunch that you'd like it too, if we found the right guy. If I found him," she finished, suddenly struck with the perfect plan.

"Maybe," he said, not sounding convinced. "How about this? You pick out your dreamy real-life Ken doll—only with a cock—and I'll meet with him. But no promises, okay?"

Instead of shaking on it, they kissed—deeply, passionately, the kind of kiss where his mouth covered hers, his teeth digging into her skin, overtaking her lips, her tongue, her essence. And then, for the next hour or so, she forgot about the other man she wanted to find, and focused on the man who truly mattered as they twisted and writhed and joined until they finally slept, curled against each other.

Rory was the type of girl who didn't waste time analyzing every available option. If she wanted something, whether a pair of sunglasses or a gourmet chocolate bar or a new suitcase, she let whichever caught her eye be the one she chose. She didn't consider it impulsive so much as decisive. When she knew, she knew, and she figured shopping for food or jewelry or accessories had to be something like shopping for men. And it kind of was, except that there wasn't a store where she could find a man who'd fuck her boyfriend and let her watch—and even if there was (she wasn't above imagining such a thing), Rory wasn't sure she'd want it to be that easy, the way online dating always promised. There was a myth that you could plug in height, eye color, race, penis size, and get the perfect man, but she knew from her own trial and error that it just didn't work like that. Men might seem easy, and some of them were, sexually, but she liked the spark, the challenge, the interplay. Or maybe she just liked men who made her work for it.

Especially for this mission, she didn't just want any man; she wanted the right one, the one who'd turn both her and Alex on, one who wouldn't simply tolerate her in the bedroom, but would get off in some way on being under her distinctly female, masturbatory gaze. Instead of the morass of online options, there was the gay bar her favorite fags had recommended, the one most open to women, where maybe there might be a bi, or at the very least, curious, guy who'd consider her offer.

She knew that this foray into fag hagdom would be different from when she'd gone to the bars just for fun, when she was the Girl, usually the only one, sometimes one of a handful. That world was theirs, and she was the outsider, a tourist, but a very eager one. She could blend, precisely because she didn't want to take home a souvenir. Here she was not a visitor, but the instigator and collaborator.

She'd decided to wear a red corset top covered with a thin white cardigan and her darkest, tightest jeans, plus heels. She knew many gay men who couldn't resist a pair of breasts looking like they'd been served up on a platter, and she loved to flirt, especially when flirting was the endgame. She could feel the puzzled glances of men wondering if she'd stumbled into the wrong kind of bar, if she wasn't looking for the one filled with punks and metalheads down the block. She let the bartender concoct her drink—"Something fruity," she specified with a wink—then went back to perusing the bar. There were men here she herself could get wet for, but she wasn't here for that. Well, not only for that. She was here for Alex, to show him what he, what they, were capable of.

She sipped her mystery drink and waited. The right man would come to her, that much she had learned from a decade of chasing boys. She was happy to observe the boys at play, especially the go-go boy in just his tighty-whiteys. Flirting with gay men had always come easy for her, but she was on a mission tonight, and she tried to look relaxed yet mysterious. It wasn't until she'd turned toward the bar, her ass sticking out, that a man walked up and complimented her. "Lady, if I swung that way, you'd be the kind of woman I'd want to take home."

She turned to find a pale, husky man, full-bellied, with a beard, glasses and short brown hair she instantly wanted to run her fingers through. Whereas Alex has a swimmer's lean body, this man clearly liked to eat and drink. He was wearing a blue sweater and had a twinkle in his eye; he was probably only a few years older than her twenty-eight but had a wise look to him.

"What's a nice girl like you doing in a bar like this?" he asked with an exaggerated accent.

She grinned at him. "How do you know I'm a nice girl?"

"Now that's what I like to hear. What are you having?"

He proceeded to buy her a drink, and as they chatted, she found herself almost reluctant to get to her point. Would he think her yet another boring straight girl partnered with a fag in disguise? Or would he get how much more complicated her situation was? It was only after her third drink that Rory truly opened up. Vince was enraptured, listening to her with his full attention, not trying to signal any of the boys or ogle anyone out of the corner of his eyes. He didn't even ask to see a photo of Alex, but he did want to know all about his personality and their sex life. "Usually, well, usually I'm the bottom. Actually, almost always. Maybe I don't look it tonight"—she indicated her top, which, while not an actual corset, still made deep breaths a challenge—"but I like to be bossed around. Told what to do. Ordered to do things I might initially balk at. But this is different. This is something I'm asking him to do for me...but not just for me, if that makes sense."

Vince put his hand on her shoulder and said three simple words that let her relax, even within the constricting top. "I get it." They closed out the bar talking about Alex, sex, and then finally, just for fun, the other men in the bar. "Alex looks kind of like him," she said, pointing, and Vince whistled. Their date was set when she hugged Vince good night.

When they were finally alone in the hotel suite Rory had picked for its elegance and discretion, sleek modern charms and most especially its California king-size bed, she realized she didn't know what to do with her hands. She was used to keeping them busy—even when they were bound behind her back. Her long nails often sported a chipped red color from all her fidgeting and busywork. What she ached to do as she looked at the two men poised before her was run her hands through their hair, clutch at their chests, dig those nails into their backs. She was used to being the center of attention with men or women, in bed or out, and this was something new. She'd requested it, but it would still take a little getting used to, staying perched in a plush chair off on the side of the room.

But tonight, Rory was there to watch. She wanted to see Alex find a new side of himself. She knew those lips, those teeth, those hands, that cock. She knew every inch of him and wanted to think she knew what happened in his head, but she could never know it all. Maybe he couldn't either.

In her head, this moment had looked like one thing: a fantasy come to life, a seduction scene par excellence. But in real life, fantasies become something more real—more nuanced, more passionate precisely because they aren't perfect. Alex looked at her and she wasn't prepared for the emotions playing out on his face: fear, excitement, lust—and thanks. He was thanking her for giving him something he hadn't even been sure he wanted. Alex was the one who was nervous, his usual toughness stripped down. She smiled at him, a tender smile, not a cruel one. She didn't want to subject him to something he would despise or even tolerate, just because she could. There'd been a time when she would have wanted that, when pushing men's boundaries made her feel more powerful, her version of digging her heel into his balls, but without the sadism. This wasn't about power, but pleasure, both of theirs.

In her fantasy, Alex had been with the consummate, six-packed, gleaming hunk, the kind blaring from billboards for gay gyms and preening from dirty magazine covers. In the end, though, who she'd chosen—and who'd chosen her, and Alex—was a real man, more real than some gymbot could ever be. Vince had hair on his chest, and arms, and back, and legs. He was big and strong and didn't say a lot, not like he had at the bar. You could call him a bear, but he had told her he didn't care about labels. He just liked to hold men down, make them cower; to turn them, not to put too fine a point on it, into girls. And that was what Rory really wanted to see, she realized, as Alex stripped in front of Vince: to switch not just places but genders, for a night. Not literally—that was too simple. He could've put on lipstick and a dress and panties, but she didn't want him as a girlie girl, but a girl like her: a tough girl turned liquid at the helm of a big strong man. She wanted him to know what it was like to submit so fully, so wondrously, that everything else disappeared.

She stepped a little closer, but not so close as to ruin the moment. "Alex, are you going to let me inside you?" Vince asked. Well, really he was telling, but a good top knows how to give an order and make it sound like a question, how to make getting what they want seem like the bottom's dream come true.

"Yes," Alex said, his voice high and strangled. Now his eyes were closed; he didn't dare look at Rory. She hoped it wasn't awful of her to get quite so wet from seeing him like that, a little helpless—not just before Vince, but his own desire. Had he buried it for so long only to now, finally, reveal it, or was it something new, prompted by all their talks leading up to this night? She didn't know, but she didn't need to. She took out a small vibrator, a discreet miniature version of her beloved Hitachi Magic Wand, and slid it up under her skirt, flush against her fishnets. She loved getting her tights wet with her juices, loved how the fabric pressed tight against her skin just where she needed it, and now that sensation was amplified. She had her girl world in the corner, while the boys explored something all their own across from her.

Rory had been to strip clubs, all but one filled with naked, jiggling, beautiful girls. She'd liked it, but could never quite get past the reality to enjoy the fantasy come to life. She'd wanted to know what they used to keep their hair in place and how much money they made and all sorts of details that were anything but erotic. The male club she'd visited with a bachelorette party had been laughably full of men so polished and preened they'd lost all their sex appeal to her. She'd forgotten what it was like to simply take pleasure in pure, unadulterated voyeurism, the kind where you're witnessing something truly intimate. That's what she saw before her now: Alex, on his knees, taking Vince's cock all the way to his big, hairy balls. The soft "Wow" escaped her lips before she even realized it.

It was one thing to picture all kinds of filthy scenarios, but quite another to see it in the flesh. Alex's eyes opened for a moment and she watched him strain to keep his mouth in place and be used in the same way he liked to use her. When his stare went on too long, Vince pulled out his dick—that Rory, an admitted size queen, was pleased to note was at least nine inches—and slapped it across Alex's face. Rory whimpered, then bit her lip and pressed the vibrator harder against her clit, then just tore the fishnets entirely because she couldn't wait. That slap was too much for her. Vince beat his meat against her boyfriend's cheeks until he was done. Unlike Alex, Vince didn't seem concerned with Rory in the least, and she recognized that as a kind of topping—of her. By showing her his indifference, by showering Alex with his erotic attention, he was reinforcing the fact that she'd never have him.

Rory shoved her fingers in her mouth, suddenly needing as many holes filled at once as she could manage. Vince bent Alex over the bed and Rory was torn between rocking against her toy and staying still to maximize the view as Vince lubed up his fingers, then jammed then into the ass Alex had only let her inside that one time.

Soon all she saw was Vince's backside, as he stood behind Alex, put on a condom and prepared to enter him. She felt like the ultimate dirty old woman as she moved to get the best view possible, but it was worth it: Alex's cheek was bent against the bed, and he looked nervous but ecstatic, and when Vince entered him, she saw right away that she'd been right. Not that

Alex was gay—she didn't care about the terminology—but that he liked it, liked having another man's cock up his ass, liked being on the bottom, liked having his body run over roughshod. Vince bore into him, quietly but intensely, and Rory lost count of how many orgasms she had as she took in the transformation happening before her.

At the end, when Vince said, "I'm going to come all over you," she stepped away. She wanted to give them a moment of privacy, and she'd seen all she needed to. She knew many women, perhaps most, might be unnerved by what she'd seen tonight, but Rory was energized, awakened to a beauty she had hoped for but still hadn't quite expected.

After Vince left, with a kiss for Alex and a hug for Rory, they were quiet, calm, each lost in his or her own thoughts. She watched Alex do little things like eat a hamburger and flip channels on the TV in wonderment. He had changed—but so had she. And yet when he kissed her, his weight pinning her to the bed, getting lipstick all over him and the otherwise-pristine white sheets, she realized that he was also the same and, most importantly, hers. Not to own or control, but to share. She gazed right into his eyes—and he into hers—as their lips met.

ABOUT THE
AUTHORS

JACQUELINE APPLEBEE (writing-in-shadows.co.uk) is a black bisexual British writer who breaks down barriers with smut. Her work has appeared in many anthologies and websites including Cleansheets, *Best Women's Erotica, Best of Best Women's Erotica 2* and *Best Lesbian Erotica.*

RACHEL KRAMER BUSSEL (rachelkramerbussel.com) is an author, editor, blogger and In the Flesh Reading Series host. Her books include the novel *Everything But* and the nonfiction *The Art of the Erotic Love Letter.* She's edited over thirty erotica anthologies, including *Passion, Fast Girls, Spanked, Peep Show, Please, Sir* and *Please, Ma'am.*

ANGELA CAPERTON's (blog.angelacaperton.com) eclectic erotica spans many genres. Look for her stories published with Cleis, Circlet Press, Drollerie Press, eXtasy Books and in the indie magazine *Out of the Gutter.*

HEIDI CHAMPA (heidichampa.blogspot.com) has been published in numerous anthologies including *Best Women's Erotica 2010, Playing with Fire, Frenzy* and *Ultimate Curves.* She has also steamed up the pages of *Bust Magazine.* If you prefer your erotica in electronic form, she can be found at Clean Sheets, Ravenous Romance, Oysters and Chocolate and The Erotic Woman.

DEVYN CHRISTOPHER (theurbanrogue.blogspot.com) is a freelance writer with a background in kink, anthropology, mysticism and seditiousness. His blog, Urban Roguery, has received numerous positive reviews, and was among the Top 100 Sex Blogs of 2009. A native New Yorker, he lives in Toronto.

PORTIA DA COSTA (portiadacosta.com) is a British author of romance, erotic romance and erotica who loves writing about sexy, likeable people in steamy, scandalous situations. Her many novels have been translated into a variety of languages, and she's had well over a hundred short stories published in magazines and anthologies.

ANDREA DALE (cyvarwydd.com) has been published in *Orgasmic, Alison's Wonderland* and *Sweet Love,* among many others. She's walked on the Charles Bridge in Prague and seen the go-go dancers, but that's all she's admitting to.

JEREMY EDWARDS (jeremyedwardserotica.com) is the author of the erotocomedic novel *Rock My Socks Off* and the erotic story collection *Spark My Moment.* His work has appeared in over forty anthologies, including *The Mammoth Book of Best New Erotica,* vols. 7–9, and he has appeared at the In the Flesh reading series.

K. D. GRACE (kdgrace.blogspot.com) lives in England with her husband. She is passionate about nature, writing (her novel is *The Initiation of Ms Holly*) and sex—not necessarily in that order.

KAY JAYBEE (kayjaybee.me.uk) wrote the erotic anthologies *Quick Kink 1* and *Quick Kink 2*, and *The Collector*. A regular contributor to Oysters and Chocolate, Kay also has stories published by Cleis Press, Black Lace, Mammoth, Xcite and Penguin.

REGINA KAMMER is a librarian and art historian. She began writing historical fiction in 2006 during National Novel Writing Month. About midway through that fateful month she switched to erotic fiction when all her characters suddenly demanded to have sex. She lives in the San Francisco Bay Area.

ALEXANDER LIBOIRON is a native of New York and currently hangs his hat with his wife in Brooklyn, with whom he enjoys an open relationship. He has been involved in the kink community for several years, and loves nothing more than meeting people with varied sex lives who are willing to share stories.

PIPER MORGAN (pipermorgan.blogspot.com) has been published in *Strange, Weird, and Wonderful Magazine, Night Terrors: An Anthology of Horror* and will have two stories appearing in *Daily Flash 2011: 365 Days of Flash Fiction*.

SOPHIE MOUETTE (cyvarwydd.com) is the pseudonym for two widely published writers of erotica, romance and speculative fiction. Sophie's first novel was *Cat Scratch Fever*. Sophie's short erotica has appeared in *Best Women's Erotica 2005* and

2007, Best Lesbian Love Stories 2009 and various *Wicked Words* anthologies, among others.

LIV OLSON is a management consultant in Raleigh, NC.

ANIKA RAY is a journalist. She was born in the Midwestern United States but now covers politics for an international newspaper based in India. In her opinion, there's nothing better to unwind with than a smart, erotic story.

KAYAR SILKENVOICE (SilkenOnSex.com) is a bisexual polyamorous writer living in San Francisco. A postfeminist graduate of one of the Seven Sisters Colleges, she hosts the weekly Silken on Sex Podcast, writes to promote sex-positive culture and produces erotic audio recordings. Kayar's passion is sexual exploration.

ALISON TYLER (alisontyler.blogspot.com) has published short stories in more than eighty anthologies including *Rubber Sex*, *Dirty Girls* and *Sex for America*. She is the author of more than twenty-five erotic novels, most recently *Melt With You*, and the editor of more than forty-five explicit anthologies.

ABOUT
THE EDITOR

VIOLET BLUE (tinynibbles.com, @violetblue) is a *Forbes* "Web Celeb" and one of *Wired*'s "Faces of Innovation"—in addition to being a blogger, high-profile tech personality and infamous podcaster. Violet also has many award-winning, best-selling books; an excerpt from her *Smart Girl's Guide to Porn* is featured on Oprah Winfrey's website. She is regarded as the foremost expert in the field of sex and technology, a sex-positive pundit in mainstream media (CNN, "The Oprah Winfrey Show," "The Tyra Banks Show") and is regularly interviewed, quoted and featured prominently by major media outlets. A published feature writer and columnist since 1998, she also writes for media outlets such as *MacLife, O: The Oprah Magazine* and the UN-sponsored international health organization RH Reality Check. She was the notorious sex columnist for the *San Francisco Chronicle* with her weekly column "Open Source Sex." She headlines at conferences ranging from ETech, LeWeb and SXSW: Interactive, to Google Tech Talks at Google, Inc. The *London Times* named Blue "one of the 40 bloggers who really count."